Sur la route

OTHER WORK BY CECILIA WOLOCH

Earth

Carpathia

Narcissus

Late

Tsigan: The Gypsy Poem

Sacrifice

Sur la route

a novel by

Cecilia Woloch

Quale Press

Strange travel plans are dance lessons from the gods.
— Kurt Vonnegut

ONE

My plane leaves for Paris in less than an hour. I'm not sure my luggage is going to hold up: a roll-aboard with a zipper that sticks; a carry-on heavy with journals and books, its straps already stretched too thin.

I've crammed everything I think I'll need for a month into these two bags.

Mid-November and it's eighty-three degrees in Los Angeles. Mid-morning and the sky's a milky blue tinged with smoggy gold.

The cab drops me off at LAX. I drag my bags through the sliding glass doors into the terminal, flooded with sunlight, already sweating under the coat I've slipped on so that I won't have to carry it.

I've checked the roll-aboard and rushed to the gate before I remember what I forgot: I don't have a way to reach Jack in Paris; we haven't made any plans for how we'll meet one another there. I find a payphone and dial the number of his house in New Mexico, relieved when I hear his voice.

"*Bonsoir*, Susannah!" he chirps. Though it's bright day outside everywhere — except in Paris, where it's dusk.

"That's *evening*," I tell Jack. "That means *good evening*."

"Oh," he says. He's coming to France in two weeks; he'll need to know how to say hello.

"Do you have a number in Paris?" I ask. "How will I get in touch with you there?"

"Call Pierre," and he gives me the number. "Pierre's English is better than Isabelle's. Call him as soon as you get to Paris, and ask him to call Isabelle. Ask him to ask her to call me here. I want to be sure I can stay at her place."

I add Pierre's number to the list of names and numbers in my notebook, a list that's grown in the past few days.

"And how will I find *you* there?" Jack asks.

"I have no idea," I say.

And then I hear my flight being called — the final call for boarding — so I pick up my carry-on, and run.

TWO

And what am I running from? Los Angeles falling away, already, beneath me — forever: too bright, too flat. My life as a stranger everywhere. The way I keep failing and failing at love. My fear of being trapped inside that shining flatness, too. Perhaps what Baudelaire described as *l'horreur du domicile*.

And what am I running toward that I've only glimpsed but keep longing for? A city with grit on its heels and the smell of tobacco on its breath. A river that glimmers, as if with stars. A world inside the world, just out of reach, more *real* somehow.

It's 1994; I've just turned 38 years old, an age when a woman in Los Angeles begins to disappear. Okay, I think, *disappear.* Close my eyes above one city; open them in another city halfway around the world.

THREE

I have this list of names and numbers and enough cash to last a month in Paris, if things go according to plan.

What plan?

On my list are the names of people I met in Paris last summer, and the names of people I've never met, the friends of friends, and the names of people whom friends of my friends have met in places I've never been.

Les amis de mes amis sont mes amis. A fragile web.

I've known Jack since 1989, when we met teaching poetry at a summer camp for over-privileged kids. Jack met Pierre and Isabelle in Indonesia two years ago. They traveled together for ten or twelve days. Now Isabelle writes letters to Jack. And Jack writes letters to me in which he says he can't figure it out: Pierre and Isabelle used to be lovers but now they're just friends. So they've told him, he says. I've never slept with Jack. Well, I slept with him once, but the bed was wide. That was the year I went to New Mexico to celebrate our birthdays, which fall on the same day in early November, thirteen years apart. This year he asked me to come to New Mexico again, but I had this trip to Paris planned.

"I won't have time," I said. "Why don't you come to L.A. instead?"

"I hate L.A.," said Jack.

So he decided he'd meet me in Paris. We'll have a belated birthday dinner and he'll have a chance to see Isabelle. A reason. A good excuse. Besides, in all his travels, he's never been to Paris.

Also on my list is the name of a man, Farouk, who's promised to put me up for the month. Or so I've been assured by *une amie mutuelle*: a woman named Karen, who I met in Paris last summer at a party of expats and French hangers-on. She wanted to stay in my L.A. apartment for the month that I'd be gone; so, in exchange, she's arranged for her friend in Paris to let me stay at his place. Farouk has a big apartment, Karen's assured me, and works long hours and is rarely at home; she's explained our arrangement to him and he's agreed to everything. "Don't worry," she's said repeatedly, though I've never spoken to Farouk.

What I'm doing, I tell myself, is what my mother calls *stepping out on faith*.

Nothing beneath me now but miles and miles of sky.

FOUR

I doze off somewhere over the dark Atlantic, wake to sunlight, the smell of coffee, the drink cart rattling down the aisle. A voice announces in lilting French that we'll be landing in Paris soon. The huge wing tilts as the plane makes a graceful turn, then begins its descent through the clouds.

FIVE

A whim, little more than a whim, and a list of names: *what brings me here.*

Because I found myself rushing through Paris last summer, thinking *I want to be part of this.* What every woman wants: to be part of such beauty, and to be beautiful, finally, still, though she's no longer young. What I've dreamt of these past six months: to be rushing again down the narrow streets, along the boulevards, through the gardens, under the shadowy arcades. Past the shop windows full of flowers and notebooks and dresses and antique clocks. Loaves of freshly-baked bread and pastries arranged like jewels. And jewels and scarves and violins. Delicate high-heeled shoes the color of summer sky. Everything touched into place. To be touched. The smells of butter and garlic and sweat. Couples kissing in doorways, under bridges, along the *quais* beside the Seine. Flocks of pigeons rising like clouds and a ragged *clochard* asking, politely, *Madame*, for *fire* to light his cigarette. Sirens and car horns, cathedral bells. Women with voices bright as champagne walking their tiny, high-strung dogs. Men who smile or sigh as I pass. The smoky cafés and gleaming *brasseries*, each like a painting one might step into, as if into another life. To be a figure in the crowd of figures the glittering mirrors throw back.

SIX

"J'y arrive," he says. *J'y arrive.*

The man behind me touches my shoulder to let me know that he's still near. We're crossing a narrow street clotted with traffic in the neighborhood called the *Marais*. He thinks I'm distracted, which I am — my first day in Paris, I've hardly slept — and he seems afraid I'm going to wander off, which I'm inclined to do.

I arrive. Almost winter here. The sky and the pavement, the pigeons — all gray. Like a black-and-white photograph. Like the faded antique postcards I've bought from the stalls along the *quai*.

"It's here," Mike says, and points to a storefront restaurant with a hand-lettered sign in Hebrew. Israeli food. I'm buying lunch. It's the least I can do, I say. Because he met me at the airport and helped me navigate the Métro and find a room in a small hotel where I'm staying *for just one night*. Just until I can reach Farouk.

The old people smoking cigarettes at a table near the door look up when we walk in, then look away. We stand at a counter and point to the dishes we want — *this and this and this* — then take a tiny corner table where we can talk above the noise.

Mike is one of the expats I met here last summer, a lawyer who left the States to live in Paris and practice massage therapy. "To follow a spiritual path," he says. I imagine him, tall and balding, walking a path through the Tuilerries in his shiny shoes, his well-cut coat. I laugh and shake my head.

"Why not just be Jewish?" I ask. Mike's eyes go suddenly small and hard, so I laugh. "Just kidding," I say.

The hummus is oily; the bread still warm.

It's Thanksgiving Day in America. Outside the plate glass window, bearded men dressed all in black, Hasids in tall hats, heads solemnly bowed, weave in and out of the throngs of well-dressed women, well-heeled businessmen, the occasional tourist stopping the flow of traffic to snap a photograph.

Yes, I think, the city looks like a black-and-white photograph of itself: the ancient buildings leaning against one another against the sky, all the shades of gray. The way I imagined, as a child, the world must have looked before I was born. As if I've fallen back in time. As if time has stopped and let me fall back, softly, into this soft gray light.

J'y arrive: I arrive. Present tense. The only tense in French I speak.

SEVEN

My room is a box at the turn of a stairway that seems to tilt in a narrow building *in the shadow of Notre-Dame.* As if the whole thing might come tumbling down. My room is so crooked and small, the ceiling so low that I almost can't stand up to undress. There's a tiny sink where I wash my face and one tiny, thin, white towel. The toilet and shower are two flights down, dark and dank and windowless. The one window in my room opens over an alley of sooty brick. There's a black telephone next to the bed, which I use to leave a message for Farouk, and a message from Jack for Pierre. I study the other numbers on my list, as if looking for a clue.

Then I lie down on the narrow bed.

EIGHT

After I've slept for a couple of hours, after I've showered and dressed again, I rush downstairs to the red velvet lobby, all faded elegance, smelling of must, to meet Mike, who's already waiting, perched on a rickety-looking settee. The thin man smoking behind the desk takes the key to my room from my hand, slots it into one of the cubbyholes in the wall of cubbyholes at his back. "You must return by one a.m.," he says. "After that, the front door will be locked."

NINE

We've been invited for Thanksgiving dinner at the home of some friends of Mike's. Or he's been invited and I've been invited to tag along. Or am I his "date"? They're American friends, Mike explains as we pass through a series of gated courtyards, each gate with its code, its intercom. As if we're entering some kind of inner sanctum, away from the clamor of the streets, through the quiet garden — too quiet, too neat.

The apartment is on the topmost floor, expensively furnished and vast, with views of the city from every window, a full-length mirror in the vestibule. My reflection seems all wrong in this place — my short black skirt and tights and sweater; my heavy, unpolished boots; my long hair a dark mass of frizzy curls. The host, when he takes my coat, runs his gaze over my body, then looks past me, quickly, as if I'm not there.

I'm seated at the far end of the table, away from Mike. On my left, a quiet Englishman. On my right, an overweight businessman from the rich, white suburbs south of Los Angeles, getting not so quietly drunk. Beer after Lone Star Beer. And how do we start on politics? "You're *so L.A.*," he tells me, pointing one thick finger at my face. He's conservative, of course, and I'm tempted to say I'm a Communist.

"No," I answer, "I'm Susannah." Light a cigarette. Shut up.

The other women are French; they sip their wine and praise the food. I try to engage them in conversation, but they *don't prefer* to speak English, they say.

TEN

By the time it's late enough to leave without seeming *impolite*, it's so late that the Métro has stopped running for the night. One of the Frenchwomen, suddenly kind, offers to give us a lift in her car. Mike has to fold his body almost in half to climb into the tiny back seat. I ride in the front seat, watching the wet streets, so I see the police car first.

"A routine stop," the Frenchwoman says, as she brings the car slowly to a stop and rolls the window down. She flirts with the officer in the short blue cape until he smiles and waves us along.

I get to the door of my hotel two minutes before one a.m., two minutes before the front door would have been locked for the night. Glad for the shabby lobby, the warmth, the desk clerk's tired *Bonsoir*. Do I have any messages?

"Not at all," he says, shaking his head.

In my room, I lean out the window, try to catch a glimpse of sky.

It's four a.m. by the time I fall asleep, keep falling, almost dawn.

ELEVEN

I dream, deeply, of losing things: a blue suitcase left behind;
a child whose hand I let slip from my hand; a house in which
the rooms keep shifting, familiar then suddenly not. That I'm
about to be married again and have forgotten to choose a
dress; that the dress I choose is transparent, too thin, and
begins to dissolve on my body almost as soon as I put it on,
becoming more and more transparent with every step into
twilight I take. Until I'm standing in an open field in the
dark wearing nothing at all.

TWELVE

Bells. Not bells. Is it morning? Where? The black phone is jangling. It's well past noon. The voice I hear is a masculine voice, deep and confident and smooth. "Susannah," he asks, "is it you?" Then, "Were you still sleeping?" And then I'm awake.

Farouk's accent is French tinged with something more Eastern, but his English is clear and precise.

"So what are you doing in Paris?" he laughs. And, "How long are you planning to stay?" Then, as if by way of making conversation, he asks, "Where are you staying while you're here?"

"Oh," I say, waking a little bit more. "I thought I could stay with you?"

There's a pause. A little too long.

"Well, certainly, for a night or two," he says, "that would be fine."

Oh, I think. Oh.

THIRTEEN

We've made plans to meet at Farouk's apartment at four o'clock this afternoon. I repack my luggage and leave it downstairs, in the lobby, behind the desk. The desk clerk on duty — a different man now — speaks French to me, then Spanish, then Italian, then English. Okay. "No problem," he says — I can leave my bags at the hotel desk all day. But my room is already booked for tonight; the hotel is completely full. "It's the weekend, you know," he shrugs.

FOURTEEN

I rush into the street to change dollars to francs, to buy coffee, to find, somewhere, a map. When I come back to the hotel to settle my bill, the man at the desk says Pierre has called. There's a number where he can be reached. I slip the note into the pocket of my coat: *Pierre vous a rappelée.*

FIFTEEN

Taking the Métro is like playing a game, or so I tell myself. Connect-the-dots, follow one of the colored lines on the map, descend underground in one place, then emerge again in a different place. It seems like luck to me, pure luck, when I exit at Étienne Marcel. Walk the few blocks; find Farouk's address. I stand at the door and ring the little golden buzzer next to his name. No one comes. I ring again. I look at the numbers over the door and the numbers on my note and they're the same numbers. No one's at home.

SIXTEEN

From a phone booth at the corner, I call Farouk's number and get a recorded message. The same message, in French, over and over again, every time I dial. I try his work number, too, but get the same message, exactly, there. By now, it's dusk and it's getting cold. I feel the first twinge of menstrual cramps. I stand in the phone booth telling myself that I'll just keep calling until he comes home. I think of hotels, and the cash I have, and who I can call to kill time while I wait. I dig the crumpled note out of my pocket and dial the number for Pierre.

He sounds bewildered, at first, and then surprised, and then he laughs. "A friend of Jack's? And how is Jack?" And how strange that I've reached him here — still at work on a Friday evening, "playing some kind of silly game on the computer," when he should have left an hour ago. And then he asks, "So what are you doing in Paris? Where will you stay while you're here?"

I try to sound casual, explain my situation, tell him that I'm sure Farouk will show up soon.

"Come here," Pierre says, sounding serious now. "It's a big place. Come here and stay as long as you like."

SEVENTEEN

I collect my bags from the hotel desk then make my way down the narrow sidewalk, across the Place St. André des Arts. A band of musicians is playing in front of the fountain and a crowd has gathered to listen, to dance. I have to push my way through the crush of bodies — *Pardon, Excusez-moi* — then lift my roll-aboard and carry it down the steps of the Métro at St.-Michel. It's rush hour, everyone's hurrying home, and I'm in everyone's way with my baggage, being swept along by the crowd. A trickle of sweat runs down the inside of my thigh — or is that blood?

Pierre has given me two different sets of directions — one for the Métro and one for the faster underground trains, called the RER — and I've scrawled both sets of directions in the margins of my map. He lives in the *banlieues*, the Paris suburbs, just outside the Periphérique. I've decided to take the Métro because I know how it works, or I think I do; I'm sure I can find my way.

I have to change Métro lines twice, but finally I see a sign for a place like one of the place names I've written down: Maisons-Alfort or Alfortville. So I pull my bag off the train behind me and bump up the stairs to the street, then stand looking around for the bus stop Pierre said would be *right there.*

But the street is dark and empty and wide; I'm someplace far on the outskirts of town. No shops or cafés or restaurants. No bus stop anywhere in sight. I drag my bag, five blocks, six blocks, past empty office buildings and shuttered stores, until I come to a phone booth in front of a Chinese restaurant.

"Stay where you are," Pierre says when I call. "I'll borrow a car and pick you up."

EIGHTEEN

The Chinese proprietress of the restaurant won't allow me to sit down inside. Not even to have a drink while I wait for Pierre. "Tables only for customers," she says. "Only for customers having dinner," though there's not one other soul in the place.

So I stand outside on the corner and wait; cars go by, some slowing down, the drivers staring at me as they pass. I wonder if I look like a prostitute. Or some vagabond, hopelessly lost. Or like a tourist, hopelessly out of place in this place where no tourists come. Standing there, alone, in my long black coat with my bags at my side, my hair completely wild by now. What am I doing here, anyway?

It occurs to me that no one I know in the world knows where I am. With the exception of Pierre, who's on his way to meet me now. I hope. A total stranger to me, but he's Jack's friend, I tell myself, most likely another aging hippie, kindly and bearded, who'll offer me tea. Although what I really want right now is a glass of wine, a cigarette.

I call Mike's number and leave a message on his machine, telling him where I'm going, just so someone will know where I am. Just in case.

NINETEEN

A small white car pulls up to the curb. The two men inside stare out at me. The man on the passenger side gets out and walks toward me quickly. I don't move.

He's lean and muscular, quick and dark, a thatch of black hair falling over one eye. He stops in his tracks and looks at me, hard. He looks confused or surprised or both.

"Is it you?" he asks.

I say nothing.

"Susannah, is it you?"

"Pierre?" I say. So it is. So I am.

TWENTY

The man driving the car is Carlos, the neighbor who lives upstairs from Pierre in the big white house, three stories tall. The house is lit up at the end of a wild, dark garden, down a long, narrow path from the gate. "It's nothing," Pierre assures me, when I thank them for having come to pick me up.

Carlos waves goodnight and disappears up the stairs at the side of the house.

Pierre lives on the ground floor, the *rez-de-chaussée*. He shows me into a large room: low-slung chairs, a low table, a couch, a gilt-edged mirror above the mantle, framed black-and-white photographs on the walls. A door to the left leading into a bedroom, I guess; a door opposite the front door, slightly ajar, leading into a bathroom; the arched entryway to the kitchen next to that.

The first thing Pierre thinks we should do, he says, is call Jack.

He dials the phone and hands the receiver to me then walks out of the room.

"Hey, guess where I am?" I ask Jack when he answers.

"Oh," he says. Then again, "Oh!" Then, "What is Pierre doing now?"

From the kitchen, I hear the sound of running water, a clatter of plates.

"The dishes?" I guess. And I guess that Pierre has heard me over the noise when all three of us laugh.

TWENTY-ONE

A half hour later, after I've *freshened up* — meaning: slipped into the bathroom, slipped in a tampon, wiped the blood from my inner thighs — there's a knock at Pierre's front door. His friend Michel has arrived for their Friday night game of chess. This is what they do *for fun*, Michel explains, an impish tilt to his grin. Pierre calls him *Mimi*; I should, too. Mimi wears little round wire-rimmed glasses, looks more *intellectual* than Pierre. I watch the two men embrace and exchange the four kisses, two on each cheek, that mean hello. Mimi pulls a bottle of red wine, like a sly thief, from under his coat; glasses appear, and an ashtray and matches and cigarettes. I sit on the couch and the men lean back in the low-slung wooden chairs. Pierre bought the chairs in India, he says. And yes, the photographs on the walls are his photographs — fishermen, old women, children — taken *on holidays in the East.*

Mimi's English is lilting and clear. We make polite conversation for a few minutes, then he looks at me and asks, "And what do you think of the new regime in the United States?" Meaning the Republicans coming to power, the recent midterm elections, a hard shift to the right, the conservatives led by Newt Gingrich and his "Contract with America." Perhaps this is Mimi's way of asking what kind of American I am.

I think of last night's drunken businessman, his finger pointed at my face. I sigh and shake my head. "It's bad for people like me," I say, "for artists and working people, and for the poor. But it's good for the rich."

Pierre and Mimi look relieved. We're all on the same side here — *à gauche*, to the left, they nod and smile. So we talk about politics for a while.

But when they slip into French, I can't follow them far. I can only tell that they're talking about a woman they know, a woman who only works part-time, whose boyfriend gives money to her when she's broke. Mimi translates: "I mean Pierre."

Pierre shrugs. "We mean Isabelle."

I start to wonder about this woman, if she's some kind of *femme fatale*. If Pierre is in love with her, still. If Jack is in love with her, too. She must be beautiful, I think, to be able to live on the kindnesses of men. As Pierre leans forward to light my cigarette, Mimi pours a little more wine into my glass.

TWENTY-TWO

Pierre and Mimi have rolled out a futon and made a bed for me on the living room floor. Pierre brings a sheet and a blanket, too, and asks if I'll be comfortable sleeping here. I must be tired now, Mimi says, so they'll leave me alone to rest. They'll play chess in the other room, so that I'll have some privacy here.

Mimi stands in the doorway a moment, then, and cocks his head and grins. "Sleep well, Susannah," he says, "and please don't worry. We'll come in to ravish you during the night." As if he's read my mind, and so my last wildest fear dissolves. I laugh and wish them both goodnight. They close the door, but I hear the sound of their voices, murmuring, soothing to me as rain.

I slip into a nightgown — silk, too thin — then slip between the sheet and the blanket, shivering, close my eyes.

Hours later, I hear the two of them saying goodnight near the foot of my bed. So close I can almost feel their breath. I pretend to be sleeping; they whisper in French. Then I do sleep, though it's cold on the floor.

TWENTY-THREE

When I wake, it's late Saturday morning and Pierre is already gone. He's left a note saying he's gone to get bread and croissants, he'll be back in a little while.

By the time he returns, I've showered and dressed, rearranged my bags to take up as little space as possible, zippered them closed.

"Did you sleep well, Susannah?" he asks. Standing at his own front door as if he's the visitor here. His jacket a mustard-colored anorak he wears with the collar turned up. A cigarette cocked in the corner of his mouth, the smoke making him squint one eye.

"Yes," I lie, "I slept very well."

"I was afraid you wouldn't be warm enough," he says. Then steps into the room.

TWENTY-FOUR

He's made coffee and pours it —pitch-black, strong — into matching large blue cups. We sit on the couch and smoke and talk, the French/English dictionary open on the low table in front of us. We lean together over the words. His breath is warm with coffee and smoke. He draws me a rough map of the town. "So you won't be lost again," he says.

Later, he shows me the way to the station where I can catch the RER; I have to walk fast to keep up with him. "The Champs-Élysées of Alfortville" — he gestures with one arm at the main street lined with small shops and Christmas lights. He gives me the key to his apartment and tells me he's going to a party tonight and won't be home until very late.

"I'll get the extra key from Isabelle," he says.

I kiss the cool air beside each of his cheeks. He stands very still and does not kiss me back.

TWENTY-FIVE

I meet Mike in St.-Cloud, an elegant suburb on the other side of Paris, where he rents a room in an elegant house in which he is not allowed to have guests. So we go for a long, foggy walk in the park. A park we don't know the history of — though there was a palace here, once; palace grounds. The wide, pebbled paths for royal carriages; the gardens laid out with such precise symmetry, though nothing is blossoming now.

The few other walkers in this mist are men who, Mike jokes, must love my boots. Meaning: the way they stare at my legs as we pass. Meaning: he's trying to cheer me up. My boots are sturdy and black and scuffed. I'm suddenly homesick, but homesick for what, for whom, for where? Or just feeling adrift in this soft, gray fog.

"A hump you'll get over," Mike says. "Just a hump." And then he says nothing and lets me cry. We sit on a bench and watch the colorless birds in the leafless trees. I don't even know what I'm crying about. I don't even know what I'm doing here.

Mike wears a hat just like the hat my grandfather used to wear — a gray fedora — when he was alive. Mike's mother is dead and his sister is dead and his father, who has a new wife, never calls. Is he trying to comfort me? He sighs. It's just that everyone disappears. That I could be anywhere, nowhere at all. In this thick gray fog in this ghostly park on the outskirts of everywhere.

TWENTY-SIX

We take the Métro into the heart of Paris, emerge in light rain on a glittering street. Mike heads for a meeting near Les Invalides; I stand in line for half an hour to see an exhibit of paintings by Gustav Klimt. Which turn out to be only sketches: women drawn naked in quick, harsh lines, their faces unfinished or half-turned away.

TWENTY-SEVEN

In the bar of the restaurant where I wait for Mike, the waiter is kind about my French, the phrases I carefully pronounce.

"Puis-je avoir un verre du vin rouge?"

"D'accord," he smiles. *"Bien sûr."*

Mike walks in, doesn't see me at first. Hunched over my notebook, writing the words, *He doesn't see me,* just as he turns and sees me there.

TWENTY-EIGHT

I get back to Pierre's at midnight. The place is dark but there's a note on the living room table for me: *Please don't lock the door, I do not have a key.* It's written in pencil, signed, *Kisses, Pierre.*

It must be three or four a.m. when I hear the soft unlocking of the door, then Pierre's voice, then a woman's voice. I open my eyes in the dark, but see only the silhouette of her hair. *Is she beautiful?* I wonder. *Is it Isabelle?* I hope. I hear them whispering, brushing their teeth. A slant of light gleams from the half-open bathroom door on the far side of the room. Then the light disappears. Then I hear the door of his bedroom close.

At dawn, I'm woken again, this time by warm dampness between my thighs; the blood I'm afraid is soaking my nightgown, already staining the sheet. I strip in the bathroom, rinse my panties and nightgown under the faucet, in ice-cold water, blooming with red. Then I wrap my wet things in a plastic bag, dig a clean t-shirt out of my suitcase, slip back into bed, wait for sleep to return.

When I finally drift off, I dream that we've all woken up together and the room is filled with light. Whoever Pierre has brought home is a friend — Mimi, or someone else I've already met. So there's no awkwardness between us, no awkwardness, after all.

THIRTY

I open one eye to peek at my watch: it's after two in the afternoon. Or my watch has stopped. Or both. I've already heard them moving around — the creak of the door, voices whispering — but pretend to be sleeping until I'm sure they've both gone back into the other room. Then I dash into the bathroom to brush my teeth and wash my face.

I'm standing in the kitchen, pouring coffee, when she appears. I've just half-turned and she's there in the doorway: a woman about my age, with gray-green eyes and tousled, honey-colored hair. We stand there staring at one another until Pierre appears at her side. At first, I think he's said the name *Heather*. "Heather?" I ask. "No," he says, "Isabelle."

Then we burst out laughing, this woman and I. This Isabelle who is not some other woman, after all. While Pierre stands between us and looks from one to the other, puzzled, then amazed. "You have the same laugh," he says. "Exactly the same." Looking from one of us to the other, as if he can't tell us apart.

THIRTY-ONE

Someone has turned up the heat, I suspect. The apartment is warm and we spend what's left of the afternoon lounging around the living room, the windows fogged with our breath. We could write our names in it; we could put our mouths to the glass and breathe, then trace our fingertips through the fog.

No one is really dressed and we stay that way — *moitié-habillé* — until almost dusk. Isabelle and I wearing over-sized t-shirts; Pierre in his boxer shorts and a robe. Drinking coffee and eating bread and looking through albums of photographs. *Here is Jack, in Indonesia; here is Isabelle.*

"Not a very good photograph," I tease Pierre. "Not as pretty as she is."

And soon it becomes a joke between us:

"Not a good photograph, I know," he says. "Not a good picture of Isabelle."

She has a gap between her front teeth, I notice when she smiles, like my mother does. She's quick to laugh and when she laughs, she laughs with her head thrown back. She rolls her own cigarettes, which I admire, and so she tries to teach me how — "Like this," she says, leaning close, licking the paper and twisting the ends. Her English is not as good as Pierre's, but her English is fine; I understand. And when they speak to each other in French, I listen hard, catch a handful of words.

"Not *normale*," they shrug, this relationship of theirs. Sitting side-by-side on the couch. They're no longer *a couple*, they say, just good friends. They're both wearing leather slippers with upturned toes, like sultans' shoes. They try to offer a pair to me, but whose would fit, Isabelle's or Pierre's?

Just before dark, I shower and dress, then leave that warm room and the two of them. I walk down the long garden path to the gate, feeling their eyes on me as I go. Feeling watched over, somehow. In light rain. The windows behind me already aglow.

THIRTY-TWO

Too impatient to wait for the bus, I flag down a cab, ask the driver in my best French to take me to the nearest Métro station. He nods, seems to understand. Then drives around and around in circles, trying to figure out what I want. Finally, he turns off the meter, takes me all the way to the Gare de Lyon for free.

THIRTY-THREE

This time, when I ring Farouk's bell, he comes to the door with the phone in his hand. Smiles at me as he might smile at a long-lost friend and says, "At last!" As if I'd lost my way and he'd been waiting for me, all along.

His apartment is spacious and modern and chic: sparsely-furnished, stark. He pours champagne and we sit down to talk. He takes off his glasses, leans forward, and looks into my eyes. A dark man, and sure of his charm. An ambitious young French-Algerian businessman, who works at a very famous hotel on the Champs-Élysées, all glamor and shine.

He's also taking my measure, I'm sure: my black clothes, my messy hair, my face, except for red lipstick, bare. "A real artist," he pronounces, as if I'm on display. Later, his hands around my waist, he'll say it again — "A real artist!" — and laugh. He'll tell me how lovely I could look with my hair pulled back, make-up rimming my eyes. Just like the eyes of a woman he loved — he'll show me the photographs — years ago.

But, for now, we discuss our acquaintance, Karen, and agree that mistakes have been made. Was she taking advantage of both of us? Farouk thinks like a rich man, I think: he thinks that other people *take*. Though he takes me to dinner — an Indian place — and insists on picking up the check.

By the time we get back to his apartment, it's too late to catch the last Métro, and a cab would cost more than the cash I have. He doesn't offer to lend me the fare, but I can sleep here, he says; why don't I stay? It's too late, too, to call Pierre and tell him I won't be back tonight.

"What if they worry," I worry, "my friends?"

"Well, they'll think you're a grown-up," he says.

So he gives me one of his clean shirts to wear, and a pair of silk boxer shorts. Asks me, "What else do you need?" He shows me a cabinet under his bathroom sink filled with bottles of lotion, cosmetics, perfume. Every luxury, every desire. I can sleep on the couch, Farouk says, or in bed with him; it's a very big bed. Then he lifts me up in his arms and spins me around.

"Though I can't promise that nothing will happen," he says. "I can't promise."

I sleep on the couch.

THIRTY-FOUR

In the morning, I wake to the back of his hand lightly touching my cheek. I like being woken like this, but I pretend not to be awake. Then the soft click of the lock and he's gone.

How light can one travel, how light?

I have, in my small leather backpack, my tube of red lipstick, my toothbrush, my comb. I put on, again, the same clothes I took off the night before: black unitard, black skirt, black boots, black sweater; scarf and coat. When I step outside, I feel almost weightless, almost as if I could just keep going, as if I need nothing but what I have.

The weather's turned breezy and clear and bright. High blue sky and gleaming spires. The sidewalks are paved like mosaics with small, white, shining tiles.

An older woman suggested this once: *Always walk as if you know just where you're going, and you'll be fine.*

THIRTY-SIX

I meet Mike for lunch on the Champs-Élysées. Then we walk down a side street, past some expensive shops, and find ourselves just across the street from the fancy hotel where I know Farouk works. The revolving glass door spins and a man rushes out. He sprints in the other direction, down the sidewalk, away from us.

"I think that's Farouk," I say to Mike.

"As you wish," he says, turning from me.

"Well, it's too late to catch him," I shrug. The last I see of Farouk: his blue jacket filling up with wind.

THIRTY-SEVEN

Mike takes me to meet his friend Marie-Christine, who lives in the 7th arrondissement, in a beautiful apartment filled with antiques, the walls lined with books. Books about mysticism, meditation, religion, psychology. From her windows on the sixth floor we can see the Tour Eiffel. She'd like to live in Los Angeles for several months next year, she's told Mike; there's a course she wants to take. Which is the reason Mike's brought me here. Perhaps we could swap apartments, he suggests — isn't that my fantasy, after all, to come back to Paris for several months? But everything hinges on Marie-Christine's divorce, so we can't make plans just yet.

And what am I doing now, she asks? I shrug. *Just being here.*

Mike has gone into the other room to phone his friend Sylvia — a young woman he also thinks I should meet. "Because she's a dancer," he says, "just like you." I've never called myself a dancer but I'm not going to argue with him.

When I take the receiver, the voice I hear sounds familiar, American, warm. Would I like to come to a dance class she's teaching forty-five minutes from now?

I'm wearing my unitard under my sweater and skirt — I could dance in that, I think. "But I don't have the shoes for it," I tell Sylvia, looking down at my heavy black boots.

"What size are you?" she asks. And of course she wears the same size shoe I wear, and has an extra pair of jazz shoes I can borrow for tonight. She gives me directions to the Centre de Dance, in the 14th arrondissement.

We're about to hang up when I mention to Sylvia that I'm looking for a place in Paris to rent, that I'm here for a month, and does she happen to know of anything? Then the whole story about Farouk comes out, and the story of Pierre — who's sweet, I tell her, but I hardly know him, and he lives so far from the center of things, and I want a place with a little more privacy, a place where I can write.

"I'm just telling everyone I meet" — though I haven't told anyone until now — "in case they know anyone who's leaving town for the holidays, or has an extra room they'd rent out cheap . . ."

"As a matter of fact," Sylvia says, "I have this studio in the 10th. And I'm living with my boyfriend, more or less, so it's usually empty now. I've been wondering what I should do with it, and I could use some extra cash."

Before I rush off to the Métro, I ask Mike how I'll recognize Sylvia. "You'll know her," he says. "She's adorable. And her hair is just like yours."

THIRTY-EIGHT

A half-dozen women are changing their clothes in a tiny, mirrored room. Which one is Sylvia? The one with the wild, dark, tangled curls. Or is that me? We turn in the mirror together and laugh. "You two could be sisters," someone says.

She's ten years younger than I am and speaks fluent French. She ascribes her "exotic" looks to being "half-Spanish, half-Mexican." She's lived in Paris for almost three years. She came here from Texas to follow a man she's since given up and has never gone back. She's who I might have been ten years ago. Who I might have become, in some other life.

THIRTY-NINE

After class, we're combing our hair with our fingers, putting on lipstick, grabbing our coats. Our plan is to walk around the corner to a café and have coffee and talk. But here is Alain, in the corridor, waiting, tall in his black leather jacket, holding his helmet in both of his hands. He and Sylvia met at a party two or three weeks ago and he's been trying to reach her since. And of course he can join us, of course we don't mind.

Sylvia draws me aside on our way out the door, whispers into my ear, "Please don't mention that I'm living with my boyfriend. I'm just kind of private that way."

FORTY

"Order anything you'd like," Alain says, as the waiter hands menus around. I order a glass of red wine, a crudité sandwich on a baguette. Alain laughs, then makes a sad face when I squeeze out the excess mayonnaise.

"You don't like our mayonnaise?" he asks.

"Too much," I say. But delicious, yes.

The *brasserie* is noisy and bright and yes, *brassy*, gleaming with brass — is that why they're called *brasseries*? We make a tableau in the plate glass window, the three of us, all in black. I think that anyone walking past might think that we've known one another for years.

Alain insists on paying the check. "I invite you," he says, and smiles. "It's a good city for women," he sighs. Then he tells us how beautiful we are.

Sylvia excuses herself and slips downstairs to make a call — to phone her boyfriend, whose name is Pierre. But not the same Pierre as *my* Pierre; we've already made sure of that.

I pass her in the hallway on my way to the ladies' room.

"Sorry we haven't had a chance to really talk," she says.

Our eyes meet in the mirror for a moment.

"No matter. Tomorrow," I wave, going past.

FORTY-ONE

And then it's late, again, and I don't want to miss the last train to Alfortville. "Don't worry," Alain says, his motorcycle is right outside. "I can take you home; it won't take long."

Sylvia nods, "Fifteen minutes, at most."

So at midnight, I'm flying through Paris with my arms around his waist. My skirt hitched up, my knees pressed hard against his hips. A blur of lights. The sign above the highway winks, PÉRIPHÉRIQUE FLUIDE. In Alfortville, we stop to ask some boys in the street the way to Pierre's address.

Alain drops me off at the gate. We kiss the four kisses from cheek to cheek and I straighten my skirt, walk down the long path through the garden toward the house.

The key is under the mat, as Pierre said it would be, so I let myself in. The room is warm; the lights are on. Pierre walks out of the kitchen, unwrapping a bar of dark chocolate. "You want some?" he asks. "Sure," I say. "Yes."

He doesn't ask me where I've been since late yesterday afternoon, but leaves the chocolate on the table, goes into his room, gently closes the door. I notice he's left an extra blanket folded on the end of my bed. A small red pillow, too.

FORTY-TWO

Morning. A match being struck. Then silence, the smell of cigarette smoke.

Well, let him look, if he wants to look.

I'm awake, but I keep my eyes closed.

FORTY-THREE

A note on the table: *There's hot coffee for you in the kitchen. Just stop the machine when you're finished. Have a good day.* — *Kisses, Pierre.*

At noon, I'm doing ballet stretches on the living room floor, wearing a t-shirt over my unitard, legs extended to either side in wide second position, when I hear the key turn in the lock.

Too late, I think, to pretend that I was doing something else.

Pierre has come home from work for lunch and to smoke a joint and relax. His job is terrible, he says — *really boring;* he had to get away.

He sits in one of the low chairs and smokes. I keep my back to him while I stretch, legs open, toes pointed, back straight, slowly pressing my chest toward the floor.

"Susannah!" he says, as if he's shocked.

"Well, what do you do, exactly?"

"Oh, it's really a stupid job." He works in an office not far from here. "I don't want to talk about it, Susannah. I'm too embarrassed."

I turn around.

FORTY-FIVE

I'm waiting for Sylvia in the Place de la Bastille in the blue hour just before dusk. I order a *crêpe au fromage* from a sidewalk vendor, sit down on a bench to eat. This is dinner; this isn't bad. Less than two bucks, and warm in my hands. I stare at the famous monument, the Colonne de Juillet, and watch the crowds as they pass.

The figure on top of the column is called "the genius of liberty." Gilded and winged, a torch in one hand. Gleaming against the darkening sky while the traffic goes around and around.

I think I see Sylvia in a phone booth; I think I see myself from behind. But when the woman with long, curly hair turns around, she isn't either of us.

FORTY-SIX

Sylvia shows up, breathless, at last. She's sorry she's late; I'm just glad that she's here. We find a café where we can talk, settle into a booth with our coats and bags. Over tiny cups of espresso, we tell stories about ourselves, to see where our stories might intersect. She came to Paris *for a man* but she's stayed in Paris for herself. I came to Paris for myself, I say — "But now there's a man?" she asks. And smiles. I don't have an answer for that.

"I'm experimenting with French men," Sylvia says, with a little shrug.

The waiter is watching us from the bar out of the corner of his eye.

I tell her a little about Pierre, what little there is to tell; that he's sweet, he's kind. He makes coffee for me in the morning and leaves me little notes. He's turned up the heat in the room where I sleep, so I won't be cold at night. And really, I'm nothing, a stranger to him. A woman who landed on his doorstep, friend of a friend half a world away. And this Isabelle, also kind, who shares his bed, sometimes, but insists they're *only friends*. "I don't know what to make of it," I say.

Sylvia says, "Well, it's *very French*. Texas was never like this," she laughs.

"Neither is L.A.," I agree.

The waiter makes a little half-bow when we slip out of the booth, leaving a few shiny coins beside the plate.

FORTY-SEVEN

We climb up from the filthy underground where the corridors smell of piss, up the littered steps of the Métro and into the littered streets, walk down the boulevard de Magenta, and around the corner to Sylvia's place.

Her studio is six flights up, *pas d'ascenseur*, so we have to keep climbing, all the way to the topmost floor. Then it's one room, tiny and dark; the tiny kitchenette in one corner, with a bathtub against the wall. But the price is right, and it's in the heart of Paris, and I can have it all to myself. "You'll have your privacy," Sylvia says. Though I'll have to share the toilet at the end of the hall with the neighbors on this floor. I'll buy flowers, I tell myself. I'll draw back the curtains from the tiny window that looks out over the rooftops of Paris and, far below, the streets.

FORTY-EIGHT

Sylvia's studio is available in ten days; she'll need that time to pack up the things she needs and move to her boyfriend's flat. So I just have to figure out what I want to do between then and now.

I have an open invitation from a friend in southern Germany. A man I met briefly in L.A. — another friend of a friend — who keeps a small apartment near his home near the Swiss-German border, near his bookshop and gallery, for visiting artists and writers. I can use the place any time, he said.

When I call him from the phone booth next to the Métro at Bastille, and tell him about my *situation* in Paris — that I've found a place to rent, starting ten days from now, but until then I'm sleeping on someone's floor — Dieter says, "Why don't you come here?"

I can take the train from Paris and he'll meet me at the station in Basel, Switzerland, and then we'll drive across the border from there. And so it's all arranged. I'll come three days from now, and I'll stay for a week.

Why do I feel I need to be anywhere other than where I am?

FORTY-NINE

Pierre has the French/English dictionary open on his lap. It's one a.m. and we're still on the couch, sitting side by side, looking things up, trying to figure out how many times France would fit inside the United States.

"I can't believe there isn't a map," he says.

Of what country?

What were we looking for, again?

FIFTY

I dream that I'm traveling with Pierre, somewhere in France, in his parents' car. Pierre and I sit in the back seat, like children; his mother and father sit up front. The car is absurdly small, a "bug" or maybe a "bumblebee" — a yellow car with a black ragtop. As we're driving through the French countryside, it becomes the American West. A canyon below, to our right: a river, and waterfalls. I'd been expecting the churning, gray-green Pacific, but this water is quick and bright, transparent and sparklingly clear. I tell Pierre that the water looks tempting, that I'd expected it to be dirty, too dirty for swimming, but it's not.

Yes, he tells me, it's perfectly safe. And we want to jump in, we can hardly wait. We're hot; it's suddenly true we've been hot for hours, we're dying to swim.

And then we're in an elegant hotel room, half-undressed, where we start to kiss. But I'm afraid of this, and run away. Then, when I try to find Pierre again, there's only a message that he's left at the desk, cool and distant, impersonal. And no mention of where he's gone. The desk clerk can't understand my French. I have no idea where I am. Outside the hotel, dusk is falling, blue and deeper blue.

FIFTY-ONE

"Susannah!" Pierre exclaims, "how do you know so many people in Paris already?" He's just walked into the living room; I've just hung up the phone. I've been making my way through my list of names and numbers, calling people I met here last summer, or other friends of friends, making dates to meet for coffee, trying to anchor myself in this place.

Still, I spend whole days wandering through the streets of Paris, alone.

FIFTY-TWO

I climb the five flights to Olivier's flat and ring the bell. Once inside, seated beside him on the little couch in the little living room — the *salon* — I tell him the story of how I arrived in Paris and found I had nowhere to stay.

"Why didn't you call me?" he says, and looks almost hurt. "You could have stayed here, of course." I met Olivier last summer, at the same party where I met Karen, and afterwards I taught him to dance The Electric Slide on a sidewalk under the Tour Eiffel. We haven't kept in touch, although we'd promised that we would.

"Things worked out fine," I say to him.

"Do you like Italian food?" he asks.

Olivier's wearing cowboy boots, which don't make him even as tall as I am.

We walk through his neighborhood, the 14th, where the sidewalks are dark and wide. Almost every shop and restaurant has already closed for the night.

But Café Modigliani is lively and candlelit. We order wine and pasta. The waiter bows deeply and calls me *Madame*. I tell Olivier what Alain said, how good Paris is to *les femmes*.

"Yes," he agrees, "it's the *égalité*." He tries to explain this to me with his hands. Palms together, as if in prayer. "Ever since the Revolution, there has been the separation of church and state." And then he pulls his hands apart, holds them out in front of me. I have no idea what he means, but I nod and think of Notre-Dame — Our Lady — which stands at the center of Paris, still.

Then Olivier waves for the waiter, smiles at me, says, "I invite you tonight."

I've lived in Paris for days on next to nothing, the same seven francs rattling around in the bottom of my bag.

FIFTY-THREE

A note: *Susannah — I don't come home tonight. I stay in Paris with friends. I hope you sleep well without me here (in the other room, of course!) — Kisses, Pierre.*

FIFTY-FOUR

One of the numbers on my list is a number for David and Adrienne Rose, a couple I've never met. Friends of a man I only met once, in L.A., two days before I left.

I'd given a poetry reading that evening at a local bookstore and, when it was over, I stood around chatting with friends. Telling everyone that I was going to Paris, asking if anyone knew anyone there. Because I'd already begun to feel anxious about the arrangement I'd made with Karen, who was there in the crowd, but seemed nervous, too.

"No," she kept insisting, "you're all set. You can stay at Farouk's."

"Well, just in case," I said. "Just in case." I glanced over her shoulder and saw a man in an overcoat, smiling toward me, not looking away.

I approached him, extending my hand. "Are you Jim?" I asked. Someone named Jim might be coming to the reading, Mike had written, to give me some tapes to bring to him in Paris.

"No," he grinned. "Do you want me to be?"

His name was Bill and he said he had friends who'd moved to Paris recently. He handed me his card and said if I'd call him, he'd give me their number. "Okay," I promised, not sure that I would.

The next night, I was packing when the telephone rang. My friend, Steve, calling to say that he had an old friend living in France; though he hadn't seen Jordan in twenty-five years, I should give him a call when I got to town. I wrote down Jordan's number and sighed, told Steve that my list was getting long, that I wasn't sure this whole trip wasn't crazy.

"Well, you know what they say," he said.

"No," I said, "what?"

"'Strange travel plans are dance lessons from the gods.'"

So I laughed and hung up and called this man Bill.

Which is how I got the number for David and Adrienne Rose.

FIFTY-FIVE

I dial the Roses's number from a phone booth along the avenue de l'Opéra.

"We've been waiting to hear from you," David says. His Tennessee accent makes me smile. "Bill faxed us to say you might be in touch. He thinks he's in love with you."

It's early evening. I've spent the day moving through crowds on the crowded sidewalks, through crowds on the crowded Métro, feeling invisible in my long black coat in the crush of holiday traffic, everyone else with somewhere to go.

"What are you doing right now?" David asks.

In fact, I have no plans for the evening, no plans for dinner, nowhere to be.

"Why don't you come by for a drink?" he says. Then — I can tell — he covers the mouthpiece with his hand, calls out to someone else in the room. Then, "Why don't you plan to stay for dinner, too?"

FIFTY-SIX

Everything's lit up for Christmas, in this rich *quartier*, with twinkling white holiday lights —the old opera house, with its gilded dome, the department store windows, the restaurants — even the pharmacies and banks have red-ribboned wreaths on their doors. I get cash from the ATM at the American Express on rue Scribe, stop to buy flowers and champagne for my hosts, then take the bus to Charles de Gaulle Étoile, get off at the stop for l'Arc de Triomphe. I make my way down the narrow streets, gazing up at the curtained windows. People are gathering for the evening meal; I can almost hear the tinkling of crystal and silver, soft laughter and conversation. The sense, just out of my reach, of *home*.

So I'm late by the time I arrive at the green double-doors and stand ringing the bell. Adrienne answers wearing an apron over her sweater and jeans, holding a spatula in one hand. "We'd just about given up on you," she grins. She leads me through several large rooms, all high ceilings and polished wood floors, and down a long hall to a small white kitchen, warm and filled with delicious smells. David stands waiting, a bottle of wine in one hand. "What took you so long?" he asks.

FIFTY-SEVEN

After we've feasted on chicken and *haricots verts*, on salad and bread, on chocolates and wine, their nine-year-old daughter is taken off to bed by their pretty American au pair — Camille, who seems miserable here, though they're hoping she'll stay on in Paris with them.

"We keep trying to introduce her to people her age, but she's not making friends."

I remember myself at twenty-five: how I never felt pretty enough, how I didn't know what I should do with my life.

David asks what I do in L.A. What it is I do for a living. *How a poet lives.*

When I tell them that I teach poetry workshops for kids, Adrienne wants to know if I happen know a poet named Max Gold?

I laugh out loud. Max was my first poetry teacher; he got me started with Poets in the Schools; he's one of my oldest friends in L.A. He's also Adrienne's cousin's brother-in-law.

"Max pulled a stunt at my cousin's wedding, walked down the aisle on the best man's arm."

"That sounds like the Max I know."

"Next time you need a place to stay in Paris," David says, "remember our couch folds out into a bed."

FIFTY-EIGHT

Midnight: crossing the Place Tristan Bernard. David is walking me to the station at the Étoile to catch my train back to Alfortville.

"You really have guts," he says, "to come all this way without even knowing where you'd stay."

"No," I say, "I just jump in. Then if I end up in deep water, I have no choice but to swim." Though, in fact, I'm a terrible swimmer. And the water in the fountain we pass is shallow and glimmering.

FIFTY-NINE

The house in Alfortville is dark when I arrive, though I'd hoped Pierre would still be awake. The door to his bedroom is closed. No note on the table signed, *Kisses, Pierre.* Though I left a note for him this morning, saying I hadn't slept well without him here, and wonder now if maybe I went too far.

I'm leaving for Germany in the morning; when I come back to Paris next week, I'll be staying at Sylvia's place. So I pack my bags and write a note: *I have a train to catch in the morning, will you please wake me up before you go?* Because I've slept late every morning, too late. Because the green shutters keep the room dim. Because the garden — so long and drenched — keeps the noise of the street far away.

I tuck the red pillow under my head, thinking he might lean down and touch my shoulder to awaken me.

SIXTY

The music is soft, at first — so soft, I barely hear it — and then it's sweet and dark and strange. A chorus of voices, angelic chords. Then bells. Then I open my eyes.

Pierre is standing across the room, near the stereo, turning the volume slowly down again, watching me lift my head. "Susannah," he asks, "do you sleep enough? Will you like to sleep some more?"

"An hour," I say. "I could sleep one more hour. But then I'm afraid I won't wake up again in time to catch my train."

It's okay, he says, he'll call me from work. And he sets the black telephone next to my bed.

SIXTY-ONE

When I leave for the station, I leave one of my bags in a corner of the living room, packed with the things I won't need in Germany, and a note that says I'll return for the bag when I come back to Paris next week. Also a bottle of champagne, a tin of coffee, a hundred franc note — "For the phone," I write on the back of a postcard of Marilyn Monroe. A black-and-white photo in which she's all innocence, in a full-skirted snow-white dress. Then I put on my lipstick, print one red kiss beneath the place where I've signed my name.

SIXTY-TWO

As I step from the taxi at the Gare de l'Est, a woman with a battered Polaroid camera snaps my photograph. Here, in this glittering late morning winter light, in front of the station, vast as any cathedral, laughing, with sky in my hair.

But of course there's a price, and I shake my head, walk away, leaving the woman standing there, cursing me in French. Calling back to her over my shoulder, "Too much, *trop cher.*" *Too dear.*

SIXTY-THREE

The rails split the landscape in half. I have to choose which side of the aisle to sit on, which half of the scenery to watch pass. And whether to take a seat facing backward, watching Paris recede, and then the rest of France; or facing forward into the green blur of fields and whatever happens next. I choose to face forward, Paris behind me, my face pressed close to the window glass.

SIXTY-FOUR

If I had to draw a map of how I've come to be on this train, I'd have to go back and back again and try to unravel the distances. And maybe it wouldn't be a map of the Earth, but of constellations, or a chart of who led to whom.

I'm on my way to meet Dieter, who I met through a man we both know, Sam, who's an artist and traveler. I first met Sam through a woman I was close to, years ago, one of several women who was in love with him at the time. I was never in love with Sam, though it was Sam who first introduced me to the man who's become my ex-husband, who is still our mutual friend.

It was my ex-husband who phoned, just before I left L.A. for Paris last summer. He'd heard I was going to Europe. Did I know that Sam was in Germany, staying with this gallery owner named Deiter? My ex thought Sam sounded lonely and bored. Why didn't I call him when I got to France? He might get on a train and come to visit me.

Which is exactly what Sam did. And he brought along a manuscript that Dieter had given to him. A memoir by a woman named Paula, who had come to Deiter's bookstore to give a reading from her book, which had been published in German, in Switzerland. Deiter wanted to publish the book in English — Paula's first language and the language she'd written it in — but the original manuscript would have to be edited first. "You should get my friend Susannah to do it," Sam had said. Which got him the ticket to Paris, I guess.

So, Sam and I wandered around Paris together for a couple of days in the summer heat; and when he left, he left Paula's manuscript with me. I read it on the plane going back to the States, made notes in the margins and waited to hear again from Sam. Instead, in September, I got a message from Deiter on my answering machine. He was in L.A. and wanted to meet me; Sam was out of town that week. The problem was, I was also out of town.

That week I was teaching in the mountains a couple of hours away from L.A. Deiter had a rental car, he told me, but would he be able to find the place? I gave him the number of my friend Anthony, who also lived in L.A., who also wanted to visit me in the mountains, but his car was broken down again. Maybe Anthony could ride up the mountain with Deiter and show him the way? The house where I was staying had room enough for all of us.

So Deiter and Anthony drove up together, thick as thieves by the time they arrived. I took a photograph of the two of them, standing outside on the deck of the house: the small, fair, middle-aged German man, blushing as he smiled, standing next to the tall, dark Chicano, scowling into the sun. That night, I burned the pizza I'd been trying to warm for dinner; we drank red wine and talked; Anthony played his harmonica. Then we each went to sleep in our own room.

In the morning, over coffee, Deiter and I talked about the manuscript. Yes, he'd like me to edit it, he said; he'd talk to the writer, Paula. He'd even see if he could find me a place to live in Paris while I worked on it. "You've charmed him," Anthony said.

Anthony is a man I've been in love with many times. When we first met, I was still married. By the time my husband and I divorced, Anthony was married to an ex-

~ 75 ~

girlfriend of my ex-husband's closest friend, a man who is also a friend of Sam's. Once, without realizing what he was doing, Sam introduced my ex to Anthony — introduced my ex-husband to my ex-lover — at one of the parties Sam was always throwing in his backyard in L.A. I only heard about it later; I hadn't been invited to the party, at my ex-husband's request. As if we could keep the past separate from the present, somehow, or the past separate from the past.

Now Anthony and the ex-girlfriend of my ex-husband's best friend are divorced. But it's never worked out between Anthony and me. Which is one of the reasons I came back to Paris with my battered suitcase, my battered heart. Because no one loves in a straight line, I think.

Which is one of the reasons I'm on this train.

SIXTY-FIVE

Five hours to Basel, where Dieter has told me he'll be waiting, so I can relax. I know where I'm going and where I'll be for the next seven days. A little respite, then, when I'll not be so *vagabond* for a while.

I have Paula's manuscript in my bag. It's the memoir of a young black woman, an immigrant from the Caribbean living in the London slums, imaginative and poor and maybe too brave for her own good. Lured by an ad that promised a job as *an entertainer* in Switzerland. But the job turned out to be a ruse. And the Swiss businessman who'd bought her train ticket had taken her passport, too. He threatened to turn her in to the authorities as *illegal* if she tried to get away. So she was forced to work as a stripper for years, until she managed to escape. Most of the other young woman in her situation fell prey to prostitution and drugs.

I check to make sure the manuscript is in my bag, and that my passport is still there, too.

SIXTY-SIX

He smiles as he hurries toward me: a middle-aged man whose long woolen scarf makes a dash of red in the station's gray. "I'm so glad that you're here," Dieter says, loading my baggage into his car. He says this over and over again, as we drive away from the lights of Basel into the darkening countryside. "I'm so glad that you're here."

Along the neatly paved winding road, between the neat little towns that look, somehow, not quite real to me, as flat and quaint as movie sets, the occasional neon sign glares: *The Pussycat, The Top Hat.* The kinds of strip joints where Paula was trapped; how innocuous they look. And where might the clientele have come from if not from these immaculate little towns?

The Swiss-German border is just ahead. Something inside me fears this crossing, as if I might be crossing into enemy territory. My father, dying slowly now on the other side of the world, fought in World War II. His older brother, John, was killed behind German lines. And so my father has hated all things German ever since. I wonder if I'm betraying him now, and what I'm doing here. Just the kind of woman the Nazis had hoped to eradicate. A little bit Jewish, a little bit Gypsy; a left-leaning poet; American.

"I'm so glad you're here," Dieter repeats, and laughs as the border guards wave us past, not even stopping the car.

SIXTY-SEVEN

Dieter's wife, Margaret, puts food on the table: brown bread, cold salmon, mild cheeses, hot tea. Then she goes off to choir practice, leaves us to talk in the quiet house. The kind of house where one takes off one's shoes at the door and pads through the well-ordered rooms in socks.

"I should tell you what's going on," Dieter sighs as he puts down his fork. The little apartment he'd said was available, that would be all mine when I came to Germany, is occupied, as it turns out. An artist showed up from Iceland and needed a place to stay. So Dieter's arranged that I'll stay with Inga, an old friend of his who he's sure I'll like. And for a few nights I'll be comfortable here, he hopes.

"I was afraid to tell you while you were in Paris. I was afraid you wouldn't come." And maybe he's right, and maybe not.

"Dieter," I smile, "that's the way this whole trip has gone. Nothing's worked out the way I'd planned. But it's all worked out fine so far, somehow."

He pours glasses of homemade wine, insists I try one of his cigars. "Well, it isn't Paris, I know. . ." he shrugs.

No, it isn't Paris. The clock in another room softly chimes. Outside, the neat little streets are quiet and empty and dark.

SIXTY-EIGHT

The next evening, there's a *vernissage* at Dieter's gallery. I'm dressed all in black, like everyone else. The white room hums and buzzes with conversation, with bright fluourescent light. A Russian man plays the accordion; everyone stands around, sipping Beaujolais. Little English is spoken here; I understand fragments of what's being said and the rest washes over me: nothing but sound. The language not sharp and barbed, as I'd thought it would be, but soothing and musical.

I step outside and follow the sound of rushing water to a stream. Stand in the shadows and listen to that.

SIXTY-NINE

On the drive back to Dieter's house, we talk quietly about love. A narrow road through the countryside. Only the glow from the dashboard, a sliver of moon, the headlights' twin beams shining ahead. Dieter asks me about Anthony — "Such a wonderful man," Dieter says — and I try to explain what's between this man and me, but it's difficult to explain. "It's not a *relationship*," I say, "It isn't *romantic*." A *friendship*, then. *An old story*, I tell myself, that changes each time it's told again.

"We should call him when we get back. Let's call him tonight," Dieter says.

So we do. It's nine hours earlier in Los Angeles, still the middle of the afternoon. I hold the heavy black receiver to my ear and say his name. I tell him all about the fiasco in Paris with Karen's so-called friend, the arrangements she said she'd made with Farouk in exchange for being allowed to stay in my place.

He says he'll call her for me; he'll even get her out of my apartment, if I want.

"I love you," I say, before hanging up.

"Yeah, me too." A long silence then.

SEVENTY

The phone rings at two a.m. I rush into the living room to grab it before the ringing wakes up the whole house. Karen sounds frantic and distraught; who is this man who called, threatening her? We spend half an hour talking long distance, trying to straighten things out. Then I give up. Either Karen was lying or Farouk was lying or both of them lied to me. "Everything's fine," I finally say. "It's worked out fine." Then I drop the receiver into its cradle and go back to bed.

SEVENTY-ONE

Sunday is a day for visiting, so Dieter takes me to meet Hildegaard, his friend who teaches English at a German junior high. Maybe I'll come to talk to her classes while I'm here? Glasses of sherry mid-afternoon, to take off the chill. Gray skies and the clanging of church bells we seem to step into when we go.

SEVENTY-TWO

We stop at Inga's to drop off my luggage on our way to meet Paula in Switzerland. Inga lives in a village called Bad Säckingen, in a large, old yellow-brick building that was a factory during the Second World War. Her apartment is spacious, with scarred wooden floors, enormous windows overlooking the station and railroad tracks. And on every surface — every windowsill and ledge, every small table and shelf — Inga has scattered tangerines and tiny foil stars. For Christmas, perhaps, which is coming. Or for the sake of her guest, who I am. Or just for the pleasure of the beauty of these arrangements of beautiful things.

Inga shows me the bed she's made up for me in this, the largest of the rooms. Tea and chocolate, then, and bread. Her eyes are sad when she smiles and Dieter touches her hand in thanks. And I think: *These are not my enemies. These are not my enemies.*

SEVENTY-THREE

Paula's waiting for us in the Zurich train station, sitting in a restaurant called The American Café. A dark-skinned woman alone at a corner table, sipping something blue. Her hair in dozens of braids, her long skirt slit along one thigh. She's beautiful. She takes my hand and tells us, please, to order anything we'd like. But Dieter insists on paying for apple pie and coffee in thick white cups. I have Paula's manuscript in my bag; she seems surprised when I pull it out and start to show her the notes I've made. She looks from the manuscript to Dieter and from Dieter to me and shakes her head. She's already signed a contract with an English publisher; they already have someone under contract to edit the original English manuscript. But she likes the work I've done, the suggestions I've made in the margins, and promises, "Next book." Dieter seems not at all upset; he flutters around the two of us, pleased to see that we've hit it off.

And why wouldn't we, after all? We're the same age, almost the same size, both small and dark and *foreigners* here, among the pale, soft-spoken Swiss. Her tangled mass of braids; my tangled mass of unruly curls. Her high-heeled pumps and narrow skirt; my thick black boots, short skirt and tights. The blonde waitress, neatly buttoned up, responds to Paula's *danke, thanks,* with a thin-lipped *bitte, please,* doing her best, it seems, not to stare.

Paula has become a kind of minor celebrity here. Her book a scandal because of what it revealed about the treatment of Third World women by the law-abiding Swiss. The flimsiness of those laws. "The hypocrisy," she says, as she shakes her head. But now, she sighs, this country is the only home she has.

SEVENTY-FOUR

Along the Bahnhofstrasse and all along the waterfront they loom: small congregations in tight knit groups around the flame, the spoon, the syringe. Dieter drives slowly and points out the sights. He tells me that this is the richest street in all the world: the gold of murdered Jews in vaults beneath the paving stones, the Christmas lights suspended above in sparkling waterfalls. We swerve and, in the headlights, a needle pierces the flesh of an arm. So close I get a faint cold taste of silver in my mouth.

SEVENTY-FIVE

The apartment building where Paula lives has surveillance cameras and multiple locks. It's a modern building, the rent is high, but it's close to the park where the junkies gather and she's already been robbed here twice.

Paula and I link arms as we walk down the brightly lit corridor; Dieter follows us, all smiles. Inside her apartment — which is enormous, and so sparsely furnished it looks as if she's only just moved in — she gestures at *all this space* she has, asks if I'd like to stay in Zurich awhile? I could live with her, she says. And we laugh. All the possible lives we could live. Within each world, another world: conservative bankers who crave *exotic* nudes, strip clubs hidden in country towns.

Paula tells me about the girls being trafficked from Eastern Europe now — from Poland and from Russia, where the poverty is worst — promised jobs or lives as pampered wives, then turned into prostitutes.

Paula offers me a pair of shoes, delicate and stiletto-heeled, my size and never worn. I look down at my sturdy black boots and shake my head, *Thank you, but no.*

SEVENTY-SIX

I wake in Inga's house to winter sunlight in every room.
Bread and coffee on the kitchen table, butter, jars of jam.
A place has been set for me: a clean plate and napkin and
cup, a knife and spoon. Inga has left a note to let me know
that she's teaching this morning, but will be home in the
afternoon.

Her dark-eyed teenage son appears from time to time in
doorways, and each time swiftly disappears.

SEVENTY-SEVEN

I call my mother in the States because I want her to know where I am. In case she needs to reach me, in case my father's condition gets worse. He's had stroke after seizure and stroke; his mind turns corners and won't come back. What would it to do him, I wonder, to think of his daughter here, in a small town inside the German border, feeling the way he feels? That the Germans murdered his brother. That this is a country of murderers. When I was a teenager, my friends who drove Volkswagens — *Hitler-mobiles,* my father called them — were forbidden to park in our driveway, and I was forbidden to ride with them.

Now my father's voice comes brokenly over the line. "I love you," he says, then repeats, "I love you" — a few of the words he can still pronounce. And then, "Where are you?" Confused again.

"I'm in Europe," I say, "near the Swiss-German border." Because I've crossed that border so many times, it's not really lying to blur the line because I'm almost hoping he won't understand.

"What are you doing there?" he asks. Then stutters, then says, "Come home."

SEVENTY-EIGHT

His name is Jonas: the teenage boy, the quiet son in Inga's house. He doesn't resemble his mother at all — who is blonde and frail, a little worn — and he seems embarrassed each time he walks into a room and finds me there. As if he doesn't know what to do with his long arms and legs, where to rest his eyes.

"He looks like his father," Inga tells me; his father who was a mime, an Israeli Jew, a man she loved. Who *did not object* to the child but refused to marry her. And she was thirty-five at the time, and she thought, would she have another chance? So she's raised her son alone. "I've never been sorry," she says.

Jonas, as in Jonah, who survived in the belly of the whale.

SEVENTY-NINE

Early evening and we're walking through the mists of Bad Säckingen. The clack of our heels on the paving stones, the quiet town even quieter now. Inga shows me the library, the museum, opens the gate to the garden square. In the dusk I can just make out the shape of the statue within: *The Trumpeter of Bad Säckingen*. A boy who looks half-angel with his horn. There's a sad, romantic story that's become a legend here: the boy loved a girl he couldn't woo and so he played a song for her. She loved him back, of course, but is that how the story ends? Did her father allow them to marry? Or did the girl become a nun? Inga shrugs and shakes her head; no one here seems to recall.

EIGHTY

The dark river is rushing past; the church bells chime: it's six p.m. We hurry toward the cathedral just as the huge wooden doors are swinging closed. An old man with a heavy ring of keys, who must be the caretaker, stops in his locking and turns to us. Inga speaks to him in German; I understand only *Los Angeles*.

And then he's turning the key again, pushing open the heavy doors. Switching on lights as we follow him into the quiet vestibule, into the aisle. He wants us to see it all: he gestures toward the gilded ceiling, the plaster angels, the sad-eyed Christ on his slender cross. The organ in its loft above the rows of wooden pews. In the reliquary, I stare at the cherished chips of bones of saints. Notice the scar on the old man's head: a jagged line across the flesh of his bare skull, above one eye.

I think of the uncle I never knew, killed in the war by German troops: my father's only brother, John, whose body was never brought home. And this old man in the church must be near my father's age, so he must have been a soldier, too. Fifty years since the end of the war. If he's seventy now, he was twenty then. I stare at him and wonder, *Are you my enemy?*

EIGHTY-ONE

The old man speaks a steady stream of German, pointing first to his scar and then to his chest, over and over again. He's speaking to Inga but looking at me, and of course I can't understand. I slip away, to the back of the church, find a chapel to Mary in the shadows, candles in red jars flickering at the feet of the blue-robed virgin, the Holy Mother, for whom the grandmother I never knew was named. My father's mother and the mother of his brother John. I don't light a candle, myself, but someone has lit all these candles, someone is praying to her — for what?

When I join the old man and Inga again, the old man is coming to the end of whatever story he's telling her, at last. The only words I understand are the words for *Christian*, and the name *John*. Inga nods her head and we thank him as we go. Out in the street, Inga turns to me and tells me what he said: *That the holiest day of the year for him is September 29th. The day he was taken prisoner by the Russians in World War II, who gave him the wound to his head, the scar. On September 29th, three years later, he was released from the prison camp. On September 29th, three years ago, the new organ he's so proud of was delivered to the church. September 29th. The day of Saint Johann, he said. Of John.*

EIGHTY-TWO

This morning, Inga's friend Dagmar will be picking me up. She sounded efficient and brusque on the phone, her English perfect, neatly clipped. "If you're in this part of the world, you must see our waterfall at Schaffhausen," she said, "near the border, in Switzerland." Also, she has some very old English books she would like me to take to the States and try to sell; I can keep a percentage of the profits if any turn out to be valuable. She needs the money for a recording of poetry that she wants to make for the blind, and she would like to meet an American poet — which, by now, I guess, I am. At first, I'd suggested that she simply bring the books to Inga's house, but she wants to show me around, so I've agreed.

At ten a.m. exactly, Dagmar lets herself in the front door. So much the woman I'd expected that I'm trying not to grin. Middle-aged, with short red hair, a long blue raincoat, sensible shoes. She carries a basket filled with books and bread, strides down the hall to shake my hand. And then we're off in her mustard-colored car through the neat green countryside.

EIGHTY-THREE

The fort above the town is a fairy-tale fort, no blood-stained walls. A Christmas wreath has been hung from the tower; there are no tourists here but us. Dagmar takes my picture against a sky full of steeples and clouds. Then we descend the hundreds of steps into the heart of the village of Schaffhausen. Typically Swiss: windows full of clocks and watches, cobblestone squares full of orderly crowds. Today is December 9th, the day of St. Nicklaus, Santa Claus. Bearded men in bright red costumes are leading donkeys down the streets; flocks of children are following them. The men are handing out little men made of gingerbread, with raisin eyes. They give one each to Dagmar and me, although we're not children, and the children in the crowd around us smile. We slip the men into our bags. "Just in case we get hungry," Dagmar says, "along the way."

EIGHTY-FOUR

We have lunch in a noisy cafeteria above a department store, where Dagmar tells me, in plain facts, the story of her life. How she left her husband of twenty years for another man, a man she'd first loved when she was a girl. How she left her daughters, grown by then, and her house. Gave up everything. Her *life*. Then gave birth to an *illegitimate* son in middle age. He's sixteen now, away at school. She has no regrets; she loves the boy.

"And what about the man," I ask, "whatever happened to him?"

"*Ach*, he married someone else. Someone much younger." She tilts her head, her features sharp and fine in this strong light, sharply etched.

EIGHTY-FIVE

Dagmar walks quickly, and I have to rush just to keep up with her. "Repeat after me," she says. "At least try." The word for *thank you* in German is *danke; bitte*, the word for *please;* and *war es* is pronounced "var ess" and means *where is*, which makes perfect sense.

Though I would prefer to be practicing French, would like to daydream about Pierre, in secret, to taste the edge of that ache. I get the feeling that Dagmar knows this, somehow, and wants to snap me out of it.

We cross a footbridge over the river, then turn back to gaze at the waterfall. The water crashing against the rocks makes little rainbows in the air, shimmering haloes of blue and green and red and golden light.

EIGHTY-SIX

"Yes," I say. And why not? I'd like to see Dagmar's farmhouse, because she seems eager to show it to me. So we drive along the Swiss-German border to the village of Berenweg, and then just beyond the village to where the small stone house sits alone on a hill.

The house is two hundred years old; it wasn't much more than a heap of stones and a run-down barn when she bought it, she says. But she needed a place to live and a place to raise her son, and so she restored this place herself. I can picture her swinging a pick, tearing down walls, then rebuilding them. The house has a woodstove, smooth plank floors, windows that look out into a garden where Dagmar grows vegetables and herbs. She has everything she needs, she says, and how simple that suddenly seems.

In the garden, she's built a small wooden house that looks like the playhouse I had as a child. A kind of summer house, with one window, a table, a chair, and a loft for sleeping above. "When you come in warm weather, you can sleep here," Dagmar says. "When you come back." Even now, in winter, so many flowers.

EIGHTY-SEVEN

Dagmar brews cups of tea for both of us from the mint she's grown and dried. We sit across from one another at her kitchen table and talk.

During the war, near the end of the war, when Dagmar was still a child, she lived with her mother and brothers and sisters in a kind of camp in the woods, with other women and their children. Hiding out while the Third Reich fell, uncertain of what would happen next. There wasn't much to eat, so her mother starved herself, she says, to make sure the children had enough. And she slept with an enemy soldier, once, in exchange for a radio, for whatever news they could get. Dagmar's father was away at the front, if he was even still alive. He'd been conscripted, she says, like all the men; he hadn't wanted to fight. "Not so unusual," she shrugs.

When her father returned, when the war was over, her mother was pregnant with the enemy soldier's child. A child she loved, but it didn't survive. And food was so scarce for so long that her mother died too young. Of heartbreak or hunger. Who knows?

Dagmar lights the lamp between us, then, and we sit across from one another at her kitchen table and read. An hour of silence as darkness falls.

EIGHTY-EIGHT

She puts me on the train at the nearest station, in Erzingen, back to Bad Säckingen. She stands on the platform while the train pulls out, not smiling, but watching me go. I lift one black-gloved hand and wave. Then open the book she's put into my lap, in German and English, a book of poems.

EIGHTY-NINE

Tomorrow I leave to go back to Paris, so I spend a last afternoon in Basel with Dieter, shopping for toys. Christmas gifts for my nieces and nephews, things hard to find in the States these days: hand-made wooden whistles, old-fashioned kaleidoscopes.

And then I spend one last night in Inga's house, with its bouquets of tangerines and stars, with its loose white curtains and trains passing by.

Everyone here has asked me, again and again, when I'm coming back. "I don't know," I tell them. "Soon." In Dieter's eyes, I've seen the eyes of the little boy who lived through the war. In Inga's eyes an old sadness, too.

There are languages I can learn, I think, by simply living among the words. *Good night* is *bitte nacht*. Though the night is not bitter; the rain is warm.

NINETY

In the morning, the zipper of my suitcase finally breaks while I'm trying to pack. So I miss the train to Rheinfelden; so Dieter will have to pick me up. And while I'm waiting for him on the sidewalk, an old man on a bicycle pedals past. Strange that he looks familiar to me, and I must look familiar to him, because, when I stare, he stares right back. It's only after he's disappeared that I remember where we've met: he's the old caretaker from the church. But it's too late to catch up with him now and, anyway, what could I say to him?

NINETY-ONE

Hildegaard's students have waited so long for me, and now there are only twenty minutes of class time left. So I dive right in, reciting poems, making jokes, taking questions from them. They're thirteen and fourteen years old; they're studying English; they're curious and young. Is there really so much violence in Los Angeles, they ask?

In the past two years, there have been riots and wildfires in L.A., an earthquake and, yes, there are gangs. But I don't tell them any of this. "Yes," I say. Simply, "Yes."

And then we toss some words around and I scrawl some words on the board and, miraculously, we've made a little poem and the students applaud. Dieter and Hildegaard beam at me from the back of the room. Then I'm gone.

NINETY-TWO

The sign on the train has been turned around: now "PARIS" shows above and "BASEL" is upside down, below. So I know it's the right train but, still, I check and check again. Dieter helps me lift my bags onto the rack, helps me find my seat, then he stands on the platform and waves. I blow kisses from the window as the train starts to pull away. This is the moment I'm starting to love the most: departure, this vanishing.

NINETY-THREE

Dusk: The Gare de l'Est is sooty and dim and filled with the smells of warm bread and piss. I call Sylvia from a pay phone to let her know I've arrived, then I flag down a taxi and ask the driver to take me to her address. It's raining; the streets are a blur of lights; the sidewalks crowded with black umbrellas; the cafés glowing as we streak past.

I've been inside those places, now, I think, on the other side of the glass. Paris seems filthy, after the Swiss-German towns, and even more beautiful.

NINETY-FOUR

Once I've stashed my things at Sylvia's place, we take the Métro together as far as the station at Montparnasse. She's on her way to meet her lover at his apartment in the 14th; she has everything she'll need for the next two weeks in her backpack and bag. "Changing places," she laughs, and turns to go one way on the *quai* as I turn to go the other way.

NINETY-FIVE

I walk through the rain down the boulevard Montparnasse, the leaves on the winter trees wet and gold, then around the corner to the little English bookstore where there's a poetry reading tonight. I'm late and miss most of the poetry, but the tiny store is packed and warm; there are people I know in the crowd. People I've met, or met again, in the past few weeks, who greet me as if I've come home. "I'm glad you're back," says Mike, who introduces me to Adele, who runs the place. She'd like me to read here with Jack next week, when Jack arrives from New Mexico. And though there's no place to sit or hang my coat, I'm swept into a chattering group and then I allow myself to be swept along to a noisy café — why not?

NINETY-SIX

In the morning I run down all six flights of stairs and into the street to buy my bread. A demi-baguette, still warm in my hands as I climb the stairs again. I make breakfast from that, and coffee and milk I warm on the hot plate, sip over the sink. *Barely room to turn around,* just as Sylvia said, but a table, a chair. A place to sit at the window and dream, and write my dreams before I've forgotten them in the traffic of voices I hear.

NINETY-SEVEN

At noon I dial Pierre's number, expecting to get his machine. It's Friday and he'll be safely at work, I think. I won't have to think of what to say. I'll leave a message about my bag and a number where I can be reached, for Jack, who's due to arrive in Paris tomorrow. Or is it today he's supposed to come?

Pierre answers the phone and laughs. He's just picked up Jack at the airport; they've just this minute come through the door. He puts Jack on the line.

"Why don't you come here now?" Jack pleads. "Why don't you just get on the Métro and come?"

I hear Pierre in the background saying, "I think she remembers the way."

NINETY-EIGHT

Pierre has made strong black coffee he serves to us, sweet, in the big blue cups. He's set out a plate of cookies, too. He can't stop laughing at Jack and me. With our notebooks and maps, our American clothes, as if we delight him at every turn. I haven't seen Jack in a couple of years, but Jack hasn't changed. His long hair is streaked with gray; his face is craggy; his blue eyes amused. Pierre takes a picture of the two of us: standing under one black umbrella in front of his house in the rain.

NINETY-NINE

His first afternoon in Paris, I've dragged Jack all over town. *Here is the way you buy Métro tickets; here is avenue Montparnasse; here is the bookstore in which we'll be reading, and say 'Pardon' as you push through the crowd.* We've emerged at the Place d'Italie, finally, searching for Chinatown, searching for the Irish bar where the friend of my friend Steve, a man named Jordan, is waiting for us. Pierre will catch up with us later, and also, possibly, Isabelle.

There's The Shamrock. There's the man with a beard at the bar, a glass of beer in his hand. I wave to him through the smoke. He introduces us to the barkeep, who finds a table for us in the back. And what do we talk about for an hour? Strangers, really, with only a common language between us, but that's enough.

ONE HUNDRED

Pierre appears at the window, knocking and waving at us through the glass. There's another man with him, Jean-Marc, his friend who's come from Marseille for the weekend, who looks like Pierre, but blonde. Jean-Marc plays the clown to Pierre's harlequin; he speaks little English, has sad blue eyes.

And so we are five: one woman, four men. Pierre makes a joke that it isn't fair. Jordan knows a good Vietnamese place that's only a few blocks away. I slip away to fix my lipstick in the tiny bathroom under the stairs. *Might as well look the part,* I think. What part? Pierre watching as I ascend.

ONE HUNDRED ONE

The restaurant is all mirrors and light, all white tablecloths and steam. We order beer, we order wine, we order dishes to pass around the big round table. *We can share.*

Isabelle shows up, at last, with Bernard, another old friend who's come to Paris this weekend, on business from Brittany. He was Isabelle's boyfriend ten years ago, before she met Pierre. He was Pierre's close friend at the time; that's how Pierre and Isabelle met. "He stole her from me," laughs Bernard. Now Bernard's married to someone else; I think: *This is how the circle expands.*

This is the first time that Isabelle has seen Jack, and Jack has seen Isabelle, since they met in Indonesia more than two years ago. They kiss the four kisses hello, then Jack sits down next to me again. He leans close and whispers into my ear, "Relax just a little bit, please. Just go with it, go with it all."

I look past Jack into the mirror and catch Pierre's eyes, watching us. He sees that I see, doesn't look away.

Everyone's chattering, English and French, telling bawdy jokes in both languages. Isabelle laughs her raucous laugh. Pierre teases me that I could turn tricks to raise money to stay in France. I crumple my napkin into a ball and throw it across the table at him. He gasps, as if shocked, and tosses it back.

And then the waiter brings us little cups of liquor, clear and strong. At the bottom of my cup, inside a glass orb, a naked man appears. And the men have women in their cups — *a tradition*, I'm being told. And because the table is circular, there isn't a way to look away. We see each other wherever we turn, and ourselves in the mirrors and, when I stand, I feel Pierre's eyes as they travel slowly from my face to my waist to my hips. So I stand there like that; I hold still.

Out on the sidewalk, we're all bundling up in the cold for the journey home — wrapping our scarves around our throats, pulling on gloves. Jack and I hang back, watching Pierre as he bends down to fasten Isabelle's zipper, then zippers her into her puffy pink coat. Her tennis shoes also pink. She smiles at him, indulgently, the way a mother might smile at her child.

"Why don't you come back with us?" Jack begs. "Why don't you stay at Pierre's with us tonight?"

"No thanks," I laugh, looking around. "Anyway, where is everyone going to sleep?" Bernard and Jean-Marc and Jack and Pierre, and maybe Isabelle, too, all together under that roof. I tell him I'm going back to my little studio to write.

"Will you be okay getting home?" Jack asks. It's midnight; the nearest Métro station is five or six blocks away.

"I'll be fine."

"She's a big girl, Jack," Pierre says, as serious now as he gets. "And she knows Paris really well."

So I wave and turn to go. In my long black coat, which I've buttoned myself.

At one a.m., I'm sweeping the floor of Sylvia's studio, shaking out rugs. It's all this dust, I've decided, that makes the place seem so dark. Though the harder I sweep, the more Paris seems to seep through the floorboards, little clouds of loosened soot. And when I shake the rug out the open window, dust flies into the dark like a shower of stars.

I wait for Jack and Isabelle at the gate of the cemetery Père Lachaise. They arrive late, with the wind in their faces, hands in their pockets against the cold. We have just a few hours of daylight to visit the graves of the famous dead.

Saturday: All of Paris out for a *promenade* among the tombs. Elderly French *mesdames* with little dogs on leashes, and young Americans searching, still, for the grave of Jim Morrison. We find the altar they've built to the rock star, though his bones have been moved, we're told. Roses and candles and poems, graffiti of lyrics on neighboring walls. Jack takes my picture under a red scrawl: *Break on through to the other side.*

By the time we find Apollinaire's grave, mostly by chance, it's almost dark. The flowers are fresh and the stone is rough; the poet died young, still amazed at the world. How can a grave be so cheerful, I wonder, so lovingly tended, and by whom? There's a poem in the shape of a heart, etched in red on the stone, in French. Isabelle opens her pocket-sized French/English dictionary and searches for the words. Squinting, a hand-rolled cigarette stuck in the corner of her mouth. Jack opens his journal and tries to copy the whole thing down, though the words are foreign to him; he doesn't even know what they mean. I run my fingers over the letters. " '*Mon coeur,*' it says," I say. "It says, '*My heart.*'" It says, " 'My heart is a flame turned upside down.'"

"Ah, yes," Isabelle nods, "very good." And closes her book.

The three of us walk the darkening streets toward Isabelle's flat, stopping for pastries along the way. We'll go to Pierre's for dinner tonight; Jean-Marc will cook, but we're hungry now. Isabelle's place is a few neat rooms on the seventh floor we climb toward, rooms full of plants and books and the last of the light and, now, jazz from the stereo. She makes coffee; she makes us at home; she rolls cigarettes while we lounge around the low table on pillows and talk.

"Did you bring your toothbrush with you?" Jack asks — in case it's too late to get back to Paris from Pierre's by Métro tonight. Of course I have. I'm *sur la route*, I tell him; I need less and less as I go. A tube of red lipstick, a pair of silk panties, my toothbrush and passport tucked into my bag. A bag I can carry over one shoulder, or across my back, so my arms are free. Lighter and lighter all the time. Soon I'll be so compact that I'll fit into almost any place, anywhere.

The three of us take the Métro as far as the Métro will take us, then walk the rest of the way. We swing through the garden gate well after dark, let ourselves into the quiet house.

Allo, allo, we call out to the empty room. Is Pierre not at home? Then I peek around the doorway and catch my first glimpse of where he sleeps. In one corner, a kind of loft with a bed above, a small sofa beneath, where Pierre and Jean-Marc are sprawled. Pierre has played soccer; his eye is bruised. Jean-Marc smokes while he watches t.v. I lift my camera quickly and snap a photograph just as I'm seen.

Just a little dinner party, Isabelle has said; just a few more friends, who should be arriving soon. "It's Paris," she shrugs. "Everyone is late."

But the kitchen looks cold from where I sit; there are no cooking smells, no sign of preparations underway. I wonder if there's going to be food, after all, and how soon? I wonder if I'll get bored and, if I do, how I'll slip away.

The five of us — Isabelle and Jack and Jean-Marc and Pierre and I — sit around the low, wide table in the living room and wait. "Do you like pastis?" someone asks, and fills each of the glasses that have appeared, suddenly, with a few inches of clear liqueur. It turns cloudy and amber when water is added, and tastes like warm licorice.

ONE HUNDRED NINE

Mimi arrives, at last, with two women, both beautiful. Diana is tall, with short dark hair; Michelle's hair is long and wild and blond. She kisses Pierre hello. I hear her murmur *Monsieur* to him. Is one of these women Mimi's date? Which? Or both? Or neither? Or whose?

The room alive now with laughter and kisses and chatter in English and in French. Space being made on the couch, and more chairs drawn up to the table, and glasses filled with amber clouds lifted in toasts to the health of us all. I look around and wonder: *Who loves whom in this room?* And then I think: *Everyone.*

They're rolling cigarettes laced with hashish, lighting them, passing them around. They're spilling ash on the table, pouring more glasses of pastis and glasses of red wine. Then, as if by magic, plates appear from the kitchen, heaped and steaming with pasta and fish. And silverware and salad and long baguettes that we tear with our hands. I'm famished by now and the food is delicious. Jack leans toward me, wide-eyed: "When did this happen?" he asks. "And *how?*"

ONE HUNDRED ELEVEN

Someone dims the lights and dessert is carried in, in flames. *Omelette à la norvégienne.* A birthday treat for Jack and me, because we're in Paris to celebrate. Sweet and sticky and hot and cold, we lick our fingers and now there's champagne, and more and more champagne. Pierre opens each bottle with a knife, with a kind of gleeful brutality. So why do I not feel drunk? So why is everyone laughing, making up new words — ridiculous lyrics — to whatever song is playing now?

ONE HUNDRED TWELVE

And who keeps turning the music up? The Talking Heads blaring from the stereo, bright and jangling: "And She Was." It sounds like an anthem, a carnival; it sounds like some dream of myself I've had.

And she was looking at herself
And things were looking like a movie

I'm looking back into the room from the gilt-framed mirror over the mantle, tilted just slightly, that holds all of us. Everyone sitting shoulder-to-shoulder and starting to sway to the music now. Everyone chiming in on the chorus, shouting together:

And she was!

And there I am in the smoky mirror, one of them — which one? — singing along. I almost don't recognize myself, at first, in the jangle and shine and smoke.

"In another minute, I'll feel like dancing," I say. And that's all I have to say. The table is pushed away, the chairs shoved back against the wall. In another minute, we're all on our feet, dancing, waving our arms in the air.

Jack and Pierre disappear, then reappear wearing only their t-shirts and bright sarongs tied at their waists. We form a chorus line, arms around one another's shoulders, kicking high, as high as we can, not letting one another fall.

The world was moving and she was right there with it
(and she was)
The world was moving she was floating above it
(and she was)

ONE HUNDRED FOURTEEN

Someone has thrown the big windows open — for air? — and now someone's leaning out of the window and someone's climbing onto their back. And then everyone's climbing up, kneeling on someone else's back. We're making a pyramid of our bodies that faces into the dark. Jack rushes out to the garden to take our photograph from afar. All of us laughing so hard we could just tumble out onto the grass.

But we untangle ourselves again, somehow, and then we dance some more.

And we're still dancing in the early morning hours.

And she was.

ONE HUNDRED FIFTEEN

At three a.m. Mimi is falling asleep across Diana's and Isabelle's laps. Michelle — who is Mimi's girlfriend this month — smiles at the three of them. Jean-Marc, slumped in a chair, thinks I'm a chemical engineer; he's overheard me quoting my high school French — *"Je suis un ingénieur chimiste!"* — and now I can't make him understand that I'm not. Pierre tries to explain by quoting his English textbook: "Billy and Betty are going to school. Billy carries a satchel!" Everyone roars. Jack, whom I've never seen as wild as I've seen him this evening, shakes his head. Pierre won't catch my eye but knows, I know, that I'm watching him.

I look around the room, falling also into their love, falling in love with all of them.

At four a.m., there are five of us left. Jean-Marc and Pierre collapsed on the couch; Jack stretched out on the futon that's been unrolled on the living room floor. Isabelle brings cans of cold Perrier from the kitchen and passes them around. Jack follows her with his eyes. I wonder where everyone's going to sleep.

This is how every party ends, with stories and with sighs. ("The last of the sexual tension," as an old friend described it once.) I'm perched on the arm of the couch and slide down so I'm sitting next to Pierre. As close as I've ever been to him, yet, and still not close enough. He makes some joke and grabs my hand; I grab his wrist and pull our hands behind my back and keep them there. Trace a circle in his palm with the tip of my finger, secretly.

But Isabelle knows. Isabelle is sitting on the floor, cross-legged, directly across from us. I look into her eyes for one long moment and think, *No*. I love this woman; I would never do anything to hurt her.

And then Isabelle stands up and laughs, steps out of her jeans in one smooth movement and crawls under the blanket with Jack. Pierre turns, smiling, to me and whispers: "Susannah, you sleep with me?" Is this a question or an answer? Who never lets go of the other's hand?

ONE HUNDRED SEVENTEEN

We have to climb the ladder up to the bed and who goes first? Pierre, reaching back for me? Or do I climb first, Pierre behind me, guiding me up and up? Once at the top, there's no room to stand, so we must lie down. I'm sure of that. And must be quiet, whatever we do, because Jean-Marc is sleeping beneath us, and Jack and Isabelle are sleeping — are they sleeping? — in the next room.

Then Jack calls out through the open door, "We've brought the dictionary to bed! The French/English dictionary is here!" And everyone's laughing in the dark. And then it's dark; there's only breath and touch, no words for this at all.

ONE HUNDRED EIGHTEEN

"Bonjour, Susannah," he says in the morning.
    "Bonjour, Pierre."
    Bonjour, bonjour.

ONE HUNDRED NINETEEN

Light slips through the shutters in warm, bright slats; everyone starts to stir at once. Jean-Marc, for a joke, takes the ladder away. Pierre calls down: "That's okay, we'll just make camp up here!" And pulling me close to him, orders, "Send up food!" Then Jack chimes in from the other room, in textbook English, as if from a script: "There is a market today in town. I will buy a cabbage and Isabelle, she will buy a carrot!" he proclaims.

Soon we're all in the living room, five of us, wearing t-shirts, still drowsy and warm with sleep; someone has made a pot of coffee so coffee is being poured. Jack looks at me over the rim of his cup. "Too much," he whispers, "too much." But I see him kissing Isabelle's fingertips, one by one by one.

Encore: *again*. Again. Pierre climbs up the ladder behind me then pins me down on the unmade bed.

"I feel like a child with you," he says.

I feel like a butterfly, wings spread. Held open, trembling in the bright air and, "Keep still," he says, "keep still."

ONE HUNDRED TWENTY-ONE

These are things he tells me, afterward, because I've asked. That all those nights I slept in the other room he lay awake and wished. That he was afraid to *faire le coup* — "I thought you were *too pretty* for me," he says. And yes, he still makes love with Isabelle, sometimes, but they haven't been *in love* for years; these days they're only *friends*. And yes, there have been *some other girls* — Michelle, last month, before Michelle and Mimi got together. And, yes, he's had the test for SIDA — AIDS — and has not been *very active* since.

My right hand open on his chest, his right hand over mine. As if to say, *Okay, no promises; just this.*

I'm lying alone with the bedclothes pulled up to my chin when Jack peeks into the room. The others are all in the kitchen, now, preparing the breakfast feast. "Can I come up?" Jack asks. I nod my head.

He climbs the ladder, lies down next to me and takes my hand and asks, "Are you all right?" I nod again.

With one bare foot I reach for my underpants, tangled somewhere in the sheets. "Do you understand what's going on?" he asks. *Does he?* I think.

I lean my head against his shoulder, whisper, "Yes."

Everyone's showered and dressed; everyone smells of the purple soap Jack brought from San Francisco, the faint scent of blackberries on our skin. In the bag I left here a week ago, I've even found clean clothes.

Jack and Isabelle and Jean-Marc have brought oysters back from the market, and lemons and white wine and cheeses and bread. "This will refresh us," Isabelle promises, as she and Jean-Marc lay out the feast. *I couldn't possibly*, I think, *It's much too early; no, I can't.*

But then how easily it goes down: the cool, crisp wine; the soft, rich cheese; the oysters that taste like sex and the sea. Everything so much easier than I ever thought it could be.

ONE HUNDRED TWENTY-FOUR

It's dusk by the time we walk down the garden path, the five of us, walking in single file. Then down the sidewalk, side-by-side, arms linked around one another's waists. We stroll the main street — *the Champs-Élysées of Alfortville!* — so slowly we miss the RER. And have to cross town to catch the Métro into Paris, after all.

Along the way, we walk past a place I don't recognize; but, "Here is the place where I first saw Susannah," Pierre remembers for both of us. Where he and his neighbor picked me up, the night I was lost and had nowhere to go. I look around, but the street seems unfamiliar and that night so long ago.

"We were going to make a sign: 'Welcome fat American girl!'" he jokes. Everyone laughs and he pulls my arm. "But you were beautiful," he says.

We take four seats and sit in pairs, knee-to-knee and side-by-side: Isabelle next to Jack, who's across from me; I'm sitting next to Pierre and he's sitting across from Isabelle. Like a kind of puzzle, the way we fit. A kind of symmetry, or luck.

Jean-Marc sits alone across the aisle and plays the exile from romance. Plays the *pierrot*, the *gendarme*, the chaperone. He's left Marseilles, Pierre has told me, because he's been fighting with his wife.

"Don't look at one another," Jean-Marc says. "It is not allowed! Look down at your shoes instead!" And we all oblige or pretend to oblige. But we can't stop laughing, can't stop touching one another and making jokes.

Pierre holds my hand and leans across toward Isabelle; Jack holds Isabelle's hand and leans across to me.

"We can look in the window," Jack suggests. "We can look at each other in the glass." And there we are, our faces reflected; the dark walls of the tunnel rushing past.

ONE HUNDRED TWENTY-SIX

My friends are *descending* at Bastille; I'm staying on the Métro until the station at République. They stand as we lurch to a stop and lean down to kiss me goodbye. I kiss them all, four kisses each. Then they're squeezing through the doors just as the doors are sliding closed. And blowing kisses from the platform, mouthing words that I can't hear, if they're saying anything at all. They're maybe pretending, just moving their lips. They stand there waving and I wave back, then Jean-Marc runs along beside the train as the train starts to pull away. I press my palm to the window as I disappear from them.

ONE HUNDRED TWENTY-SEVEN

By the time I get back to Sylvia's studio, I have twenty minutes
to change. Twenty minutes to somehow transform. Refresh
the lipstick I've kissed away. Rummage in my suitcase for
something *appropriate* to put on. I've promised to come to a
dinner party at David and Adrienne's place tonight. I think
of their elegant apartment and wish I had something classy
or prim to wear. But all the clothes I've brought are black
and a little the worse for wear. I change three times; I look
the same.

David kisses me at the door; he calls me *sweetie*. Adrienne smiles. We sip *apéritifs* in the living room. *Another world*, I tell myself. Through the French doors, I can see the table, set with good white china; the heavy crystal chandelier; the warm, bright order of this place.

The party tonight is for an acquaintance of theirs who's lived in Paris for years, an American woman who's moving back to the States, and we're waiting for her; she's late. There's also a woman dressed in gray, with short gray hair, who speaks English in neat, clipped syllables and won't look me in the eye. And a young man whose name is James — invited, I'm sure, for the au pair, Camille. A British student of economics, he shows David's and Adrienne's eight-year-old daughter magic tricks while Camille toys nervously with her hair.

When the guest of honor finally arrives, we all sit down to a lavish meal: pasta with garlic and broccoli, chicken with rosemary, wine and bread. And, for dessert, bananas Foster drenched in warm caramel sauce and *crème fraîche*. We're so sated, by then, and so tipsy, we're taking pictures of our shoes. We're toasting with champagne the slender woman who's leaving Paris, toasting wherever she's going next.

At midnight we're slipping into our coats, exchanging kisses at the door. James offers to walk me to the train, the au pair having already gone to bed. The other women go on ahead, walk in front of us, don't turn around: the guest of honor, the woman in gray. Their names have flown from me all evening and now they hurry, arm-in-arm. So that by the time we reach the steps leading down to the Métro station, they're gone.

James asks if I'd like to walk awhile? We can see the Arc de Triomphe from where we stand, the monument bathed in golden light. He loves to walk in Paris at night, he says, and the night is balmy, for winter, and clear. And because I'm saying *yes* to everything, I say *yes* to him.

We start at the top of the Champs-Élysées and make our way down the boulevard. All of Paris still awake at midnight, it seems, and out for a *promenade*.

James points out the things that have changed since he's lived here — three years now — and the things that have recently appeared: there's a McDonald's, a Baskin-Robbins, the Virgin Records Megastore. But further along, near the Place de la Concorde, where the crowds have thinned and the street is dark, the elegant embassies loom behind gates. "Here's your embassy," James says, while the guard looks askance and waves us on. And then we're walking under the arches of the rue de Rivoli.

There's a hotel lobby I have to see, there's the Place Vendôme, there's La Madeleine. And here, at last, the vast dark Louvre, the courtyard empty at one a.m. We take chairs at the balcony café that's been closed already for hours, and sit there in silence awhile, staring out at the old fortress walls. And then we're crossing the great smooth paving stones, our footsteps ringing out, emerging from the shadows where the river gleams beneath the bridge. We lean at the railings of the Pont des Arts, watching the wild ducks on the Seine. Behind us, on the benches, pairs of lovers twine and kiss.

And then it's two or three a.m. and we're standing in front of Notre-Dame. Where Paris began; we've walked that far. And all the while we've talked and talked, the night slipping by in the common tongue. History, politics, war and art. Now we're in the Marais, only four blocks from where he lives. "Would you like to come up for a drink?" he asks. I thought I'd be fast asleep by now. Instead, it's going to be dawn before I close my eyes. Again.

Three crooked flights of crooked steps, a crooked door, three rooms aslant. A bottle of gin pulled straight from the freezer, because he's *a proper Englishman.* We smoke each other's cigarettes and sip our drinks; I cross my legs. I think of how I love these conversations that go on and on and on. The French *surrendered*, he insists; they just *rolled over* for the Nazis, saved their gorgeous monuments. Paris like a woman who survives to be loved again.

James walks me out into the street at four a.m. and hails a cab. Perhaps we'll meet in London. Or New York. Or not again. He tells the driver, in French, where to take me. I slip into the back seat, don't look back.

ONE HUNDRED THIRTY-ONE

Light through the curtains, pale as milk. I watch morning creep across the roofs of Paris, sitting at the table in my nightgown, too-thin, silk. Finally alone, again, in my little studio, at dawn. Trying to write down everything that's happened in twenty-four hours. In a book in which some pages are already filled and others are blank. I scrawl my name across the white expanse. Oh sweet illegible.

These are the plans we made yesterday, which already seems so long ago: to meet at three o'clock this afternoon in front of Notre-Dame. I've slept past noon and now I'm late and, somehow, I've gotten lost: Paris swirling around me, traffic and crowded sidewalks and fog. Finally I ask a man in the street, *"Excusez-moi, monsieur, où est Notre-Dame?"* He laughs and points: there are the spires, just ahead, poking out of the mist. All I have to do is walk in that direction now.

In the big open square in front of the ancient cathedral, Isabelle stands, alone, staring up at the grand façade. I kiss her hello and ask, "Where's Jack?" And just as I sit down beside her on a low wall, Jack appears: coming out of the church in a swarm of tourists, putting his camera back into his bag. And then, from behind, two cool hands are placed softly over my eyes; a warm kiss is planted on my neck.

I turn around; Pierre is crouched like a gargoyle above me, next to Jean-Marc. "We were waiting for you," Pierre says. "We were spying from the café across the street; we watched you come." I fall back into his arms. And Jack, halfway across the square, snaps this photograph of us.

ONE HUNDRED THIRTY-THREE

In order to visit St. Chapelle, we have to pass first through security gates at the Palais de Justice, then file past the guards. Pierre sings an old American song, slightly off-key and under his breath, *I fought the law and the law won.*

The chapel, itself, might be beautiful in sunlight. Possibly. Like *the interior of a jewel* that the guidebooks all describe. But this gray afternoon the stained glass windows are opaque; the place is dim. The vaulted ceilings and gilded cherubim seem stiff and silly, dull. "Just another rich man's church," I tell Pierre, "for the rich man's god." He touches my breast through my sweater. *I fought the law and the law won.*

ONE HUNDRED THIRTY-FOUR

The courtyard of the Louvre, at this hour, is blue and echoing.
Too late to visit the museum, but we can pose by the big glass
pyramid that's lit up now from within. I take out my lipstick
and paint my lips, then pass the tube to Isabelle. "Let's do
something wild," she says. So we lie back against the glass
wall of the pyramid, spreading our arms so our fingers touch.
And Jack takes our photograph, or Pierre. And we all pose
again and again but all of these photographs will be blurred.
Double- and triple-exposures, superimposed, so we look like
ghosts. Save one picture of Isabelle and me, faces pressed
cheek to cheek, the same scarlet smile on our lips.

ONE HUNDRED THIRTY-FIVE

Because we're walking arm-in-arm, the four of us — Pierre and I, Isabelle and Jack — and Jean-Marc is walking alone ahead, wearing that jacket of Pierre's, the mustard-colored anorak, which makes him look like Pierre from behind, I break loose and rush to catch up with him, slipping my arm through the crook of his arm. Because anyone could be anyone. The sleeve of that jacket: familiar, warm.

Isabelle leaves us at the Métro at la Place du Palais-Royal. She has an appointment to keep, she says; she'll meet us later, again, at Pierre's. We stand at the top of the stairs of the station, watching her disappear.

Then the four of us duck into a café along the rue de Rivoli. I know what I want, order *café crème*: a half-filled cup of strong, black coffee; my own little pot of warm, frothed milk. "I want that, too," Jack says. *The same.* Pierre and Jean-Marc order espresso; the air in the room is thick with smoke.

Jack leans across the table to whisper, as if to conspire with me. What he wants to know is if I'm planning to go Brittany with them. A trip that Isabelle and Pierre have been planning for weeks. They'll rent a car; they'll visit friends who live not far from the Côte Sauvage. Even before I left for Germany, they had invited me along.

"I don't know," I tell Jack. "I'm not sure. I was thinking of going to London this weekend instead."

Jack looks disappointed; Pierre, sitting next to me, rolls a cigarette, pretends not to have overheard.

He stands on the sidewalk, staring across the street, dragging hard on his cigarette. I'd started walking ahead with the others, but now I've circled back to him. "What's the matter?" I say. "You look sad."

"That you don't come to Brittany with us." He takes my arm; we start to walk. "I don't want to impose myself on you, Susannah. Is that the right word, *impose?*"

"I'll think it over," I assure him. And wonder how soon I'll have to decide. And what I'm choosing between, after all. What I'm afraid of. What I want.

ONE HUNDRED THIRTY-EIGHT

We're retracing the steps I took last night. The very same route, in reverse, that I followed with James until almost dawn. So I point out the Place Vendôme to them, the American Embassy, all the sights. "You know Paris better than I do," Pierre exclaims, then asks, "Why is that?"

"I just love this city," I shrug. As if love explains anything.

The traffic spins madly around the obelisk at the Place de la Concorde, so we run. All four of us holding hands, dodging the speeding cars to get to the center alive. Here's the spot where the guillotine stood, where Marie Antoinette was relieved of her head. We hang our coats and bags on the spikes of the golden-tipped fence that surrounds the *place*, stare up at the hieroglyphics etched into the sides of the obelisk.

Before us, the glittering Champs-Élysées stretches out toward the glowing Arc de Triomphe. I take a photograph of Jack smoking a hand-rolled cigarette.

When I look at this photograph, months from now, it will look as if the tip of that cigarette set the world on fire — the boulevard blazing into the distance, the Christmas lights smeared into golden flames — all one bright blur against the growing darkness. Because, when I lifted the camera, I breathed.

As we walk up the Champs-Élysées, Jack slips his arm around my waist and whispers into my ear. "I need some time alone with you," he says. "We need to talk about all of this." I think it's Jack who needs to talk, but I agree: we need time alone.

So we decide that, tomorrow night, we'll have our birthday dinner, at last. We'll excuse ourselves from the others, just for one evening; we make a pact.

Straight ahead, the Arc de Triomphe rises, majestic, framing its own dark blue window of sky.

Jean-Marc has prepared another meal for all of us at Pierre's: salmon baked with lemon, tiny potatoes, asparagus. And Isabelle has returned to us, as promised, by eight o'clock. Jack raises his wine glass and announces: "There is no jealousy in France!"

When we've had enough wine, we sip whiskey; grow tipsy and drowsy and drift toward bed. Jack and Isabelle take the futon, *as usual*, in the living room; Jean-Marc, the couch in the space beneath the loft; Pierre and I will sleep above, again, so up we go.

When I lay my head against his chest and close my eyes, I see carousels. Glittering lights and carved white horses, rising and falling and rising again. There should be music, I think, and there is. Though the only sound I can hear is his heart.

ONE HUNDRED FORTY-TWO

Monday morning and, by the time I wake, almost all the others are gone. Pierre to work, Isabelle and Jack to wander through museums. Which only leaves Jean-Marc and me; the last of the strong black coffee; his little English, my small French. I know it's time for him to return to his troubled marriage in Marseilles, and I think his wife would be a fool to let him go, but I don't tell him that. Instead, I write down his address. As if we'll meet like this again. His hair still wet from his morning shower and mine still tangled with the warm breath of his friend.

ONE HUNDRED FORTY-THREE

I'm meeting Jack at Shakespeare and Company Books, where Ginsberg is reading tonight. But I'm late and the famous poet has already finished when I arrive. I spot Jack in the throng in front of the bookstore, searching for me in the crowd.

"I'll introduce you to Ginsberg," he says, so we stand in the line for autographs, although I don't have a book to be signed. Ginsberg's hands are surprisingly soft, as are his eyes; he wears a bright red woolen scarf looped around his neck. He seems unimpressed when I tell him I read his poems in schools, to little kids.

But wherever I look in the crowd that's milling around in the little square in front of the bookshop, I see faces I recognize. An American poet I met here last summer. An Australian architect who seems pleased to see me, but not surprised. "When did you get back, Susannah?" he asks, and, "Aren't you living in Paris now?"

The restaurant Jack and I finally choose, after an hour of wandering the streets and looking at menus in restaurant windows, is a tiny place on the Île St.-Louis, the island behind Notre-Dame. An expensive *quartier* that looks more like a postcard of Paris than Paris to me, picturesque and immaculate.

So, an extravagance of candlelight, a little dog sleeping near the door. Jack sips his wine and tells me the story of the last crazy woman he loved: the dazzling blonde he *tried to save*, he says, who made a fool of him, broke his heart. I tell him about Anthony, in L.A., who's still not sure, after all these years, what I am to him; who's been sometimes my lover, sometimes my friend, but never both at once. "What's the *matter* with him?" Jack asks, which makes me smile and shake my head.

We barely speak of Isabelle, or of Pierre.

Cher means *dear*, as in *expensive*, also *precious*, *rare*, *beloved*.

ONE HUNDRED FORTY-FIVE

This is how Jack describes how the city looks to him at night: *like a jeweled blossom opening; like a dark-skinned woman, jeweled, slowly stripping off her veils.* He stands amazed at the Hôtel de Ville and allows me to see it through his eyes: the glittering fountains; the stately building bathed in a soft, warm amber glow.

These are the gifts we've given one another: for him, a sturdy cup from Germany in which to brew his tea; for me, these dangling earrings made of glass, the light in them.

ONE HUNDRED FORTY-SIX

I spend part of each day in solitude, secretly taking back the hours. Trying to translate into language whatever's happened, what's happening now. Trying to clear a space inside myself of all the other selves. Until there's just one woman, writing in a borrowed room, alone.

ONE HUNDRED FORTY-SEVEN

This evening we're all having dinner at Isabelle's; she's making a feast for the four of us. I climb the stairs to her apartment, which is filled with soft jazz, again, and loose pillows, and delicious cooking smells. Jack and I sprawl around the low table in the living room, sipping wine. Isabelle appears then disappears to check the food. Pierre arrives and collapses, breathless, at my side. Jack makes a toast.

And later, after the meal has been served, after everyone has kissed, Jack will raise his glass again and say, "Too much! Too much food and too much wine, too much beauty, too much love!"

I'll also raise my glass and make this toast with him: to *much*.

Pierre has borrowed someone's car and so we're driving home alone. Back to his flat in Alfortville. Just the two of us, for once. We sit by lamplight in the living room and talk quietly for an hour. Perhaps we say too much. When he tells me he's fallen in love *many times before*, with *many girls*, I close my eyes. *Okay, so I'm just another fling. Well, I've thrown happiness away with both hands all my reckless life.*

I'm in my black lingerie, in tears, when he climbs up to lie down beside me in bed. "Susannah," he says, "I don't understand," and begs me, "Please explain." So I must separate the words from all the meanings I invent. And speak in simple sentences. And not disguise myself in them. And he pulls me to his chest and says, "That isn't what I meant. Oh, Susannah, it's only the language." Black silk falling. Silence then.

ONE HUNDRED FORTY-NINE

What have I dreamt that has helped me decide? Or surrendered in sleep to this look in his eyes? When I say, "I've decided I'm coming to Brittany," and he turns to me, laughing, and sweeps me up into his arms.

What have I dreamt that has meant, *Be swept away; be swept along?*

ONE HUNDRED FIFTY

I find it again: the little Irish bar in Chinatown, where Jordan
is waiting for me. From there, we take the bus to his *pied-
à-terre*, just off avenue Daumesnil. A small apartment he
keeps in Paris for the nights he works too late to get back to
his place in the countryside. Six flights up: two rooms and a
bath. "It's not much," he says, but I can use it whenever I like,
when he's not here. I'll be coming back to Paris, won't I? As
if he's sure of something I'm not. I'm exploring possibilities,
I tell him, taking in the two dark rooms with an eye toward
how I could brighten them.

Because I'm thinking already of how soon I'll have to leave, thinking already of how I'll get back — this spring or this summer, perhaps. Thinking I'll want a place of my own to live in Paris, at least for a little while.

I call Mike's friend, Marie-Christine, to propose a plan to her, a puzzle I've pieced together by which she could come to Los Angeles to start her course and share my apartment with me for a month, while Mike stays in her place near les Invalides; then, when Mike returns to the States, I'll come back to Paris and take up residence at Marie-Christine's place, while she stays on in my L.A. apartment to finish her course. I've thought this through carefully: it's a good plan, I think, and everyone's rent will be paid.

When I mentioned this idea to Mike, he laughed; he said, "Sounds good to me."

Now I'm telling Marie-Christine, but she's not saying much; she hesitates. Her divorce has been delayed, she says; she'll have to rethink her plans. And why, she asks, sounding surprised, doesn't Mike want to stay where he's living now? I tell her that his landlady doesn't allow him to have guests, that he's not really comfortable there. And then the silence on the line becomes uncomfortable, too long.

"Do you know his landlady?" I ask.

"She's my sister," Marie-Christine says.

ONE HUNDRED FIFTY-TWO

The reading is this evening, so I've gathered up my poems. I've washed my hair and put on lipstick and a dress, my good black pumps. I'm meeting Jack and Isabelle at the bookstore, and Pierre.

We all converge at the door — Pierre has brought a friend along, a quiet woman named Marie, who he thinks should hear my work — and then we all spill inside.

Mike sits at a table on the far side of the room. He stands up when he sees me, stares at me coldly, begins slowly putting on his long, dark overcoat. Buttoning each button deliberately, picking up his hat.

"We didn't even know if you'd show up tonight," he says.

As if I'd miss myself. I stand before him. Accused of what?

"Adele said you never brought the poster for the door." Adele is his friend who runs the bookstore and café. I've stopped to see her several times; I've brought Jack in to meet her, too. Now she stands in back of Mike. She shakes her head, lifts up her palms.

"Let's go downstairs," I say to him. "Let's go downstairs and talk."

And there, among the shelves of used books, he spells out the charges against me; he lists my crimes. I've ruined everything, he says, rushing ahead with my crazy plans. Marie-Christine has called her sister, and told her what I said — that Mike doesn't like living in her house — and now she's upset and he needs to find another place to live.

"You've fucked things up for me. You remind me of myself five years ago —"

I stop him there; I don't want to hear his amateur psychoanalysis, I say. I'm only human, we all make mistakes. And why didn't he warn me that Marie-Christine and his landlady were sisters when I proposed the plan to him?

Just then Jack comes down the stairs and demands to know what's going on.

"Stay out of this," Mike says. "It's none of your business."
He's seething now. I think the books are going to fall; I think
a fist-fight might break out. Jack has stepped between me
and Mike and pulled his shoulders back. But I tell Jack that
it's all right, that I can take care of myself. He turns around
and leaves, and Mike turns also, follows him.

And now I have to go upstairs and face the crowd and
read my poems.

ONE HUNDRED FIFTY-FOUR

Leaning against the walls of the tiny room and sitting in folding chairs: almost everyone I know in Paris now, and can call a friend.

I sit down next to Adrienne and whisper into her ear.

"Don't worry, hon', it's not your fault," she says. "Don't take that shit from him."

Mike has left; Pierre won't look at me and I can't look at him.

Jack reads first. He reads a long poem. I can't listen, can't concentrate. Then it's my turn, but the words all feel like stones inside my mouth. I read one poem and then another, then look up and see Isabelle. She looks right into my eyes and smiles. And Adele, standing at the back of the room, is brushing tears away. This is my work, the loose pages in my hands. This is all I've ever done, this is all I ever meant to do.

ONE HUNDRED FIFTY-FIVE

Afterwards, there are ten of us crowding into the restaurant. And room for just that many — one long table, already set — as if they'd been expecting us, though we haven't called ahead. *Bonsoir. Bienvenue.* Pierre touches my knee underneath the table, smiles and asks, "May I invite you?" And I laugh and I accept.

We eat and drink, passing bottles of wine up and down the table, baskets of bread, our plates. In France, one says *offrire* to mean it's on the house, a gift: the sweet kir served in glasses shaped like flames, the little bowls of honey candy that arrive with our *café*. And for dessert, Pierre insists that I must try *profiterolles:* vanilla ice cream in flaky pastry covered with warm, thick chocolate sauce. So rich that I can't finish, offer half of mine to him.

ONE HUNDRED FIFTY-SIX

When we're alone again he asks if he can see my manuscript of poems. Turning pages as he leans against the heater while I wait. I can't be sure how much of what I read tonight he understood. "Susannah," he murmurs, shaking his head, "what are you doing with someone like me?"

I take the pages out of his hands and kiss his mouth, lean into the heat.

The nightgown I wear to bed is thin and watery, pure silk.

"Gauche caviare," he teases. A phrase used to mean *on the left, but rich.* What he thought when he first saw my nightgown hanging on the back of his bathroom door: "Ah, she must be *gauche caviare.*"

"But it was a gift," I tell him. "A gift." The way it slides down over my hips and falls so easily to the floor.

ONE HUNDRED FIFTY-EIGHT

The quiet talk in darkness of *no protection* that first night. My fear of pregnancy and, "Why didn't you *say* something?" he asks. Just the right time to make a child, not the right time, it never is. "So we must choose a name," he says. "Should it be American or French?" And holds me close to him 'til morning, doesn't ever turn away.

"Allez!" he says; I recognize *aller*, the verb *to go*. But in which tense is he using it? He has to hurry me back to Paris to pack my bags for Brittany. To pick up Jack and Isabelle. He has the rental car outside.

I love this waking up not caring if my hair makes up its mind. Which way to go. Leave it to him. The dream I dreamed that we were traveling — how many nights ago? And now we are. It's the imperative. *"Allez,"* he says. *Let's go.*

ONE HUNDRED SIXTY

Dizzy traffic in the streets of Paris. The start of a long holiday weekend, and everyone's trying to escape. We spend an hour snarled on the Périphérique, then, at last, hit the open road. I ride in front, next to Pierre; Jack and Isabelle are curled up in the back seat, whispering. The car is red. We laugh; we sing.

And when I doze off, leaning my head against the window, I dream us back and forth in time — how terrible it was that he didn't love me years ago, how terrible the future, when he won't love me anymore. And then I wake and stop myself. Look at his profile; see my mistake. There is only this blurred present, after all. There is only this small history of kisses to his neck.

ONE HUNDRED SIXTY-ONE

On the horizon, out of nowhere, Chartres Cathedral rises up. It seems to float above the rolling fields: a ship with wings, a crown. Its spires pierce the flat gray sky. It looms, and then it seems to grow in size as we approach: white stone by stone and yet as delicate as breathing, human breath.

ONE HUNDRED SIXTY-TWO

Until it's right in front of us.

We park in the lot below the cathedral and take the steps up through the town, two by two, two at a time. Then push the heavy doors aside. As we step across the threshold, an angelic hymn begins. Pierre turns to me: "Susannah, I arrange this just for you."

Jack and Isabelle have disappeared and who knows where they've gone?

My eyes adjust to the darkness first, then to the rosy light within. The glow of candles, the stained glass windows turning evening sky to jewels. I've read that, in times of war, the people of Chartres removed each window, pane by pane. So that no war would shatter them. And saved this altar where the Virgin Mother cradles her dead son. The figure of a woman bowed and weeping and unbowed.

It's clear that this is her cathedral, everywhere I turn. Instead of heavy crosses and blood and thorns: forgiveness, mercy, love.

I have to slide into a pew and close my eyes, tilt back my head. He slides in next to me and asks, "Susannah, are you sad?" I shake my head. He understands, or seems to understand. He walks away to let me cry in peace — not far, but far enough.

The priest is chanting now in French. Pierre stands listening intently, like the boy he must have been. Like the boy who was an altar boy, he's murmuring along. I touch his shoulder and he turns to me: "You see, I don't forget." The years he spent among the monks when he was so young, just a child. Ten years old, and sent away from home to seminary school. What do I know about this man who was that boy, who takes my hand? Who walks with me around the dim circumference of the church? We pause before each niche that holds a statue of a saint, and he pantomimes the prayers he must have prayed to make me smile. He's that boy again, or still: who grew up on a farm in eastern France, the youngest child of nine, the one his mother sent away, hoping he'd someday be a priest. No wonder he's so wild. And so I don't let go his hand.

We reach the brightest alcove — Mary's chapel —where we stop. At least a hundred candles burn. At least a hundred hearts, red valentines, are set into the walls. He slips some francs into the box, takes one white taper, adds a flame to all the other flames, a prayer to all those prayers. When he comes back to where I stand, he whispers in my ear, "I've lit a candle for us here."

And then we're standing at the center of an ancient labyrinth. Gold-colored stones set into the floor in a circular pattern, a kind of map. The stones worn smooth by all who've walked this maze or followed the path on their knees. At the center, the shape of flower, or what looks like a flower to me, where we stand. We face the altar and Pierre begins to hum the wedding march. *If I carry him inside of me*, I think, *then I accept*. His child, the child he was, some part of him: I'll carry it.

ONE HUNDRED SIXTY-THREE

Outside again, I lift my camera; this time I finally capture him. I know I have; he knows it, too. This is how I'll remember him. This is the photograph from which he'll still smile back at me for years. His dark eyes softening the moment that I turn to him, surprised.

We drive in moonlight toward Nantes. The little towns of Brittany, in shadow, flying past. We're on our way to Isa's mother's — *Isa* here, not *Isabelle*. Because we've known each other long enough to use our childhood names. What has it been, now — seven days? — since we struck this fragile balance between moving, holding still?

She's the kind of woman who wears long, dangling earrings, bracelets and rings, while she cooks. Who kisses everyone hello and offers drinks; wine and cassis. Jack has never tasted kir, this taste of blackberries, before. He's amazed at everything: at Isa's mother, who smokes yellow cigarettes and speaks only French. At the apartment crammed with antiques and years of *souvenirs*. At the way the four of us sit on purple velvet chairs and don't explain. Pierre has pulled me onto his lap; Isa's mother smiles at us. She loves him, clearly — anything he does; he clearly loves her, too.

"We're just angels here," Jack whispers to me, "sent to check on them." I can't smoke the thick Gauloises. I can't agree with him, not yet.

We leave Isa with her mother in Nantes and drive the last few miles to Blaine. To Bernard and Guenièvre's *house* — there's no word for *home* in French. Though the old stone farmhouse in the middle of a field looks like a dream, like someone's dream of home, or mine. The windows gleam with yellow light; the wooden door is painted blue.

Bernard greets Pierre and Jack and me with kisses, with laughter, with a wink. I think he knows what's happened in the week since we saw him last, that night at the Chinese restaurant, before what we're calling the *fête des sarongs*.

And another friend from this crowd of friends has come to meet us here. A man named Patrick, who remembers Jack from their time in Indonesia, when Jack first met Isabelle and Pierre, whom Patrick has known since their days in school. *The world is small*, I think, as Patrick kisses me hello, as Jack throws his arms around this slight man, saying, "Good to see you again!" Patrick also knows, I suspect, also winks at Jack and Pierre and me.

In a huge room that's kitchen and living room, both, a fire is blazing in the fireplace; a meal has been prepared — *un pot au feu* — and there's champagne. A long wooden table has been set. Two small boys are playing on the floor. Antoine is four years old, I'm told, and plump Henri is one. And Guenièvre, their mother, who has slipped into the room, is pregnant with a third child, keeps one hand on her abdomen. She doesn't smile. She doesn't speak English — she barely speaks at all — and disappears before the meal is served to put the boys to bed.

So the five of us — Pierre, Patrick, Jack and me, and Bernard, who ladles out the stew — sit on benches at the table, raise our glasses, make our toasts. I'm next to Pierre but it's been hours since last we touched or kissed. I ache from that, and I'm tired, and I wonder where everyone will sleep.

ONE HUNDRED SIXTY-SEVEN

In the middle of the night, I feel the child's dark eyes on us. When I look up, I see Henri standing at the far end of his crib, at the far end of the long room lit by moonlight, quietly. He's peeking over the bars at us, where we're sprawled across the bed. Pierre, who doesn't wake. And this woman the child doesn't know, who's staring back at him.

ONE HUNDRED SIXTY-EIGHT

Morning here means everyone in various states of undress. I wear the silk nightgown and a cardigan, my hair in one loose braid. Pierre wears boxer shorts, a t-shirt, tears the fresh bread with his hands. Coffee has been made; we help ourselves. Patrick, in a robe, is rolling a cigarette as Jack comes down the stairs in a pair of sweats. This one large room holds all of us. Bernard zippering Antoine's coat. Guenièvre wiping Henri's nose. I catch her watching me from the corner of her eye — warily, I think — as if I'm dangerous to her.

ONE HUNDRED SIXTY-NINE

Later, Pierre and I shower together: I wash his hair and he lathers my back. We kiss while the water runs over us, warm, and we kiss 'til the water turns cool.

ONE HUNDRED SEVENTY

I find a window ledge in which to sit, as alone as I can get in this house, with my notebook, and fill one page. The names of the towns we've passed through; the names of the people we've met.

Jack, across the room, is watching me, holding his pen aloft. "Are you writing all of this down?" he asks. "Will you promise to send me your notes?"

And then he's aiming his camera; behind me the green fields go on and on.

We go in three cars to la Côte Sauvage — the Savage Coast — to a seaside town. We walk the misty streets, eating *pain aux raisins, pain aux chocolat*. Buying postcards to send to ourselves. Waiting for Isa to arrive. And when she arrives, she doesn't rush first to Jack, but opens her arms to the laughing Antoine. "Just look at them," Jack says, shaking his head. "Just look at them."

It's called *sauvage* because the sea is silvery and wild, because the light is savage, fierce. And we look wild in it, and beautiful, this late silvery afternoon. We stand on the rocks and pose for photographs. My hair, almost red in this strange glow, whipping against my face.

But there's only an hour of light like this — an hour or less — then the sun will set. This kind of radiance can never last; we'll never remember it.

Pierre pulls me close to him in the wind, points to the place where sea and sky seem to meet in a thin blue line. "Your country is over there," he says. My country. Whose eyes are wet?

ONE HUNDRED SEVENTY-THREE

"Tell me a secret," he says, because we're alone for a little while, driving along in the little red car. "Something you've never told anyone else." I try to hold onto his hand while he drives. I tell him about the dream I had — how many weeks ago now? — in which we were traveling somewhere together, about to make love, and I ran away and then I couldn't find him again. He says, "I do not like this dream at the end. I intend to forget the last part." When he has to change gears, his hand slips from mine.

ONE HUNDRED SEVENTY-FOUR

At dusk, we're in another ancient town, behind castle walls. Then we're buying salt — "The best salt in all of France," which is harvested here, from the sea — from the back of an old red pick-up truck at a makeshift roadside stand. We're the first customers of the day, and the last, the man selling salt says in English, in French. So we buy as much as we can, gifts from the sea for our mothers and friends.

ONE HUNDRED SEVENTY-FIVE

In the evening, we sit at the long wooden table in Bernard and Guenièvre's house, drinking cider, eating *galettes*. Bernard and Isa, at the stove, are taking turns making the Brittany *crêpes*. I forget to remember and then I remember that Bernard and Isa were lovers, once. How fluid their movements are around the stove, how almost synchronized. Isa comes to the table, the pan in one hand, leans over Pierre and slides the largest *galette* of all onto his plate. A *crêpe* stuffed thick with *fromage* and *jambon*, with *champignons*, and made just for him. Everyone applauds. Pierre kisses her cheek and, laughing, digs in.

Then Isa looks at me over his head and bursts into her cackle, which spills into mine. "They have the same laugh," Patrick murmurs, amazed, to whomever is listening. I raise my hand to slap Isa's palm; "Private joke!" we exclaim, in unison.

Everyone laughing, now, around this table in this room in this house that must glow like an island of light from afar in the midst of the darkening fields.

And we dream that we'll travel; we dream out loud. We'll rent a car when they come to the States. A red convertible, perhaps, and we'll drive with the top down all the way. "I'll have to cut my hair," I say.

Patrick looks startled, then serious: "No," he says, "get a different car." And Pierre takes my hair in his hands, pulls me close, kisses me hard on the mouth.

We've agreed ahead of time how we'll excuse ourselves tonight: I'll go first, then Pierre will come. "I must go to bed," I announce, standing up. It's already two a.m.

"We follow you," Patrick says.

"No, *I* follow her," Pierre corrects.

Down the long hall to the room where a child is already asleep in his crib.

ONE HUNDRED SEVENTY-SIX

It's possible to make love so quietly that a child never wakes.
So that the breath of the child can be heard in the darkness.
So that, much later, all the breathing in the room becomes
one breath.

ONE HUNDRED SEVENTY-SEVEN

"You haven't written much this weekend," he says. Before we left Paris, I told him that I'd want some time to write while we were here.

"What would I write?" I ask. "*Here I am in Nantes. I am eating and drinking and having sex in a room where a baby's asleep. I like this weekend very much.*" And I can't make a single poem of it.

ONE HUNDRED SEVENTY-EIGHT

Sunday is market day in Nantes, so there's fish to be bought, and cheese and wine. Jack wants to photograph every stall: the shining vegetables, the vivid fruit, the old men in their caps. The air smells like everything, and wet. I get lost somewhere between the smell of melting chocolate and the smell of bread. I'm found, again, with my hands in my pockets, standing right where they left me, after all.

In Patrick's flat, there's just room enough for one long table, the chair that each of us pulls up. We're seven now, or nine, counting the children in the laps. Counting Guenièvre, who sits next to Bernard today and smiles. There are platters of crabs boiled whole, of shrimp and oysters, and escargot. And bottles of cold white wine, and port, and loaves of bread we tear. I wouldn't eat anything still with its eyes in its head in L.A., but here I eat everything. I watch Antoine snap shrimp after shrimp with his little fingers and suck the heads. I offer Henri bites of bread. Pierre cracks the shell of a crab and scrapes out something coral with his knife. "The best part," he insists, and insists on feeding me from the blade.

Everything tastes of the sea and flesh. And underneath the table, Pierre's hand is on my thigh. His fingers cool and rough against the warmest of my skin.

Later, Antoine, licking his lips, carries in the big pink box of *gateaux*. Tiny cakes for everyone, and still champagne, and still black coffee in the fragile china cups. The cups of Patrick's dead great-aunt, to whom we toast. I raise my cup. And Isa, across the table, raises her cup to mine. "I'm glad I know you, Isabelle."

"Me too," she laughs, "I'm glad."

Jack looks at Isa — her tousled hair, her sea-gray eyes — then he looks at me and asks, "Are you all right?"

"I'm fine," I say. "A little drunk."

He shakes his head. "A little drunk and very beautiful."

The other men are speaking French and Patrick's winking at Pierre. "So you lost a week? Too bad." So I know he knows the story, too.

Then, finally, we're all taking photographs, and kissing, and being kissed. There are tears in Bernard's eyes. "I hope you return to France," he says.

"I hope so, too," I whisper back.

When at last we're piling into the car — Jack and Pierre, Isa and I — I look up from the street to the balcony. There are Bernard and Patrick and little Antoine, all in a row, blowing kisses to us. They wave and wave as we drive away until we're gone from their sight, and they're gone from ours.

ONE HUNDRED EIGHTY

We're following the moon, which is full tonight above the road. I'm wondering who I'm more in love with here, Pierre or Isabelle. I'm thinking of what Pierre said when we stood on the rocks at la Côte Sauvage: "You're so independent, Susannah. I like you this way. Don't ever change." And how once a man who claimed to love me said, "Don't ever leave my sight." And how my laugh, like Isabelle's, has a thin bright edge, a sharpness, too.

We stop for cigarettes, gasoline, to buy *café noir* from the vending machines.

"Just like America," Jack and I sigh. The lights are fluorescent and harsh; everyone needs to pee again.

"It's human, Susannah," Pierre says to me. The life of the body a life of its own. He blows his nose and I try to teach him another silly American word.

"Booger?" he asks. "Like Humphrey Booger?" And then we're laughing so hard that we're spilling our coffee. And how can we be hungry, already, again?

But in Alfortville, at last, the kitchen seems cold and sad. It's midnight on Sunday night. And there's nothing to eat in the house and nothing to drink and we're so tired.

We've dropped off Isabelle and Jack at Isabelle's place near Place de la Nation. We've dropped our bags at the door, still packed. I've promised to stay here, with Pierre, though Jordan has offered me the use his *pied-à-terre* while he's gone. "I think he's a bad man," Pierre has said. "Maybe a dangerous man. I think it's better you stay with me."

I'm going back to the States in a week; both of us know there isn't much time.

We've dropped our arms at our sides and all pretense of not being afraid.

And then, getting ready for bed, I'm surprised to discover a small stain of blood. So it's true what he said to me days ago: "It's not so easy to get pregnant, you know." So I think he'll be glad when I emerge from the bathroom and make this announcement to him. "Guess who's not pregnant, after all?" But he doesn't look relieved. He looks down at his shoes and lights one last cigarette and doesn't say anything.

ONE HUNDRED EIGHTY-THREE

This is the story he tells me, my very own fairy tale, in bed:

"Once upon a time," he says, in the middle of the night, "an American girl came to France. And she was lost." And I am lost.

"What happens next?" I ask. He gets onto his knees, spreads his arms like wings.

"Then here comes the hero, Susannah. I am the hero. It's me!" And falls over me and whispers, "To be continued . . ." into my hair.

ONE HUNDRED EIGHTY-FOUR

I dream that I'm Cleopatra, that monuments are being raised in the city of which I'm queen. A city as white as bone, and clean and wide, with blue, blue sky. I dream that I'm queen of this and that I've never had to die.

ONE HUNDRED EIGHTY-FIVE

In the morning, we pick up Jack at Isabelle's in Paris and drive him to the airport in Orly. Périphérique fluide, the electronic signs all wink at us. We kiss Jack goodbye in front of the terminal, then he turns away from us with his bags and the doors slide apart, taking him in.

When someone's gone, there's not much to say, so we turn on the radio, hum.

We've returned the red rental car in Paris so we're taking the train back to Alfortville. "We're poor again," Pierre announces, and we skip down the station steps holding hands. And sitting across from each other, knee to knee, I think: *This man is another language. How do I know him? How do we speak?*

We have lunch at the kitchen table and lay out our plans for the day: I'll go to Paris this afternoon, while he goes to work, then we'll meet and have dinner here. "I'll cook for you," he says; we'll watch an old movie on video.

"You pick up the kids and I'll see you at seven," he laughs. *D'accord. Ce soir.* 'Til then.

ONE HUNDRED EIGHTY-EIGHT

I'm meeting a friend at Café Beaubourg, the café where he spends all his afternoons. A glamorous place near the Pompidou, full of intellectuals and the *literati*, or those who wish they were. My friend is writing a book. The friend he's brought along is a young Italian director so perfectly handsome I wince. And the woman who joins us is Russian, a recent divorcée, just learning French. A few tables over, a famous writer is letting his coffee cool. We pretend not to notice him.

Everything gleams here, even the well-balanced cups, even the coffee spoons. Even the cream-colored leather chairs that reek of money instead of sweat. But my tights are torn and my bootlaces are frayed and I find myself disagreeing with everyone. No, I don't like the Postmodernists, or the New Formalists, or the English Romantics, or the work of that man over there. The author in tweed slowly lighting his pipe. I've never finished one of his books. Suddenly restless, suddenly craving Pierre's humid rooms, the real weight of his hands.

ONE HUNDRED EIGHTY-NINE

He kisses me at the door as if I've been gone for a very long time. Or as if I meet him each evening like this. As if we're a long-married couple and this is the way I come home every day. Throwing my arms around his neck, dropping my bag, being swung in the air. He kisses me at the door as if I'd left him and, miraculously, unexpectedly, returned.

The dinner he promised me: chilled Beaujolais, scrambled eggs with tomatoes, cheese and bread. "It's delicious," I say, and it is, though he laughs; it's exactly what I want. Perhaps it's the freshness of things, or the richness of the butter, or his hands in the taste of the food. He bites his nails; his palms are rough; his fingers are salty and sweet to my tongue.

Later, we feed one another chocolate, lie in his bed and watch an old black-and-white movie on television called *Freaks*. A twisted romance, a story of love and jealousy and revenge. In the end, the heartless woman is transformed into a freak. And the freaks are just as cruel. We try to decide *what it all means* while we feed one another little squares of sweetness, piece by piece.

ONE HUNDRED NINETY-ONE

This is the body of Pierre, who is thirty-two; I'm thirty-eight. And this is the way our bodies fit: his bare chest hard against my breasts. The years of soccer have made him muscular and lean, and the years of work on his parents' farm, every summer, at harvest time. His skin is smooth as stone and my skin is a river next to it. And this is the way we sleep at night: my head on his shoulder, so I can hear his heart, the steady thrum of blood. And this is what I wish: *Let nothing harm him; no harm come.*

ONE HUNDRED NINETY-TWO

Sometimes, in the middle of the night, I get up to write, and he doesn't mind. "It's *normal*," he always says — to piss, to sleep, to need time alone. Or, "As you wish, Susannah," and puts it all back into my hands.

"It's just my ritual," I've said, "like a musician who practices scales." But the truth is I'm writing now because I want to hold onto him. The man asleep in the other room. Where I am not. Who keeps me warm.

Mid-morning, he slips away from work and meets me back in bed. I'm still asleep, so he climbs on top of me and kisses me awake. He's made fresh coffee and bought croissants; he smells of his clean shirt and aftershave. *Stay here*, I want to say, and stay and stay. And never leave this room. And never have to go.

Tonight I have a dinner date with Isabelle. Just the two of us, for once. I've spent the day beginning to pack. I leave Pierre's apartment at six o'clock, just before he's due home from work.

I'm taking two sweaters that won't fit in my suitcase to give to Isabelle. I've noticed she's worn the same sweater and jeans over and over these past few weeks. Though she always looks perfect to me, she looks like a painting of herself. Or like a photograph. But not. "Do you think she's beautiful?" Pierre has asked. Whatever *beautiful* means. I think she looks, in every setting, as if she knows where she belongs. Wherever she goes, she's Isabelle.

And me, I'm already thinking, soon I'll be nothing between them again. The space they've opened for me in their lives will simply close again when I'm gone. The way those sliding doors closed behind Jack — already, then, taking some of it back.

The Métro is crowded; it's rush hour; warm. A blind accordion player gets on, then a woman who holds a poodle like an infant in her arms. I have to bite my lip to keep from crying, to keep from laughing out loud.

We have the whole restaurant to ourselves, an Indian place called le Palais d'Archana — *palace of the arcane?* The owner seems to know Isabelle. The waiter bows when he brings our food. The plates are heavy. I eat too much. It occurs to me that I'm trying to weigh myself down; it's already too late.

We talk about men and the freedom we need; we talk about our mothers and language, a little bit about Jack. And even less about Pierre, who she tells me *can only love beautiful girls.* She tilts her head and smiles at me. That gap I love between her teeth. The way she lifts her shoulders when she's sure of something, shrugs.

I tell her I'd like to really learn French, and wonder how that might change my poems. Like taking a lover changes a marriage, we agree. A lot. Not much.

By the end of the meal, by the tea and the anise seed we sprinkle into our palms, we've talked about women as lovers, too. Women as lovers and as friends. We look at each other straight on, then, both refusing to look away. If there were a switch in our hearts, she says, love would be simple: we'd simply be able to turn it on and off. She's not in love with Jack, she says, though she loves him; she's glad that he's gone. Happy to have herself to herself again, her own rooms, her solitude.

I ask if she wants to come to L.A., suggest we could swap apartments, or lives.

"You can live my life and I'll live yours," I joke. "You can have my lovers, too." Isabelle laughs, "Can I see them first?"

We walk back to her apartment near la Place de la Nation in the dark; I pick up the bag I've left here, leave the two sweaters for her. She insists she'll just keep them until I come back, but I think about Isabelle wearing my clothes and find that I like the thought. Pierre slipping my sweater over her head, maybe wondering who it is he's making love to, which one of us, or both? Or have she and I been making love to one another, all along, through him?

ONE HUNDRED NINETY-SIX

The *place* at Nation is a circle with a monument at its center, pricking the sky. The traffic goes around and around it, the little traffic there is at this hour. I feel as if I'm going in circles, too, wondering how I can circle back to this place. Pierre hasn't asked me not to leave. But he drew a map for me, once, and now I know the map by heart.

In Alfortville, I leave the deserted station, walk alone toward his house. A man is jogging in the street at one a.m.; he turns around. Asks me something in French. I tell him, *"Je ne comprends pas."* Which isn't true: I do understand.

ONE HUNDRED NINETY-SEVEN

The door's unlocked and one light's still on, though he'd told me he wasn't going to wait up. When I let myself in, he calls my name — "Susannah, is it you?" So I go into the dark room, find him in bed, dangling one arm down from the loft to me, reaching with one warm hand.

And will I climb up, please, to lie next to him? he asks. Though I still want to write and I'm not at all tired. Though I've been thinking the whole way here that I've been nothing important to him. All the *beautiful girls* he's loved, only another *adventure* to him. Though I've wanted one great love to erase a whole history of pain.

But suddenly none of that matters at all. Or that I'm bleeding. Only his mouth. Only the flesh and breath and murmured hungry struggling out of clothes. Until I'm as naked as he is. Until he's blotted out my loneliness with kisses for a while.

"What did you talk about?" he asks, having noticed how quiet I've become.

"Not about you," I say, to tease him. He looks surprised and pleased, then perplexed and hurt, and then he asks the same thing again: "What did you and Isabelle talk about?"

And I answer him, "Not about you."

So he teases me back, kissing my belly: "You have eaten too much."

And then it's time to get up and staunch the flow of blood between my legs. I wash and slip into Isabelle's robe — I've always assumed that the pink robe is hers, that the red one hanging next to it is Pierre's, though the robes are otherwise exactly the same and I've seen him wearing both.

When I lie down with him again, the robe falls open. He touches my breasts. I wonder if he knows which woman I am. If I know, myself. If I could just as easily be Isabelle in this warm bed with him now. As she will be, again, when I'm gone. They'll fit back into place; the place I've filled between them that was not an emptiness. And because I sometimes forget where I am, I say his name out loud. *Pierre.* To remind myself that I'm still here. That the world holds all of us.

ONE HUNDRED NINETY-NINE

I spend my last day in Paris going everywhere in the rain. To bookstores, to cafés, to say goodbye to everything. To tell these friends that I'll be back, perhaps in the spring; that I'll keep in touch. And then I'm on the train again, hurrying back to Alfortville. Having promised Pierre that I'd be there in time for our dinner date.

More than any other picture, this is the picture I love of myself: a woman rushing to meet her lover. Though no one has taken this photograph. And if there were such a photograph, it would be rain-streaked; it would be blurred.

TWO HUNDRED

He has a bottle of champagne chilled and doesn't mind waiting while I change. While I slip into heels and a skirt. When I bend from the waist, I can feel his eyes on my legs, almost a caress. How beautiful we are when it hardly matters anymore. He's clean-shaven and smells of soap; I wear red lipstick and perfume. We face one another and laugh. Then I let myself fall into his arms. We hold one another and sway, or the room is swaying. Almost a dance. And then I move against him, harder, close my eyes.

Can't look at him.

In the Chinese restaurant, I am called *Madame*. I am asked, "*C'est bon, Madame?*"

"*C'est bon,*" I smile; it is. Pierre's ordered dishes he knows I love — *crevettes*, asparagus — and wine. He likes to watch me eat, he says. And there's always so much to eat and drink, and so much left to say.

Then he tells me the story of his sister's death from anorexia. He wants to know if I think I'm fat? "No," I say, and for the first time in my life, "I think I'm perfect as I am."

He tells me that Isabelle called him at work today, to find out how I was. To make sure I'd gotten home okay the night before. "She's really in love with you," he says. And she told him to *take care* with me, that *Susannah is delicate*.

And then he wants to know if I think I'm in love with him.

"Sometimes I think I am," I say. "And sometimes I think I'm not." Which is the answer that he wants?

"Don't cry, Susannah, you're a big girl. Don't make your American face at me."

At the end of the meal, the waiter brings us clear liqueur in the magical cups. The liquid burns my throat going down. But there's no naked man at the bottom of my cup. There's only the glass orb, a flower, my face.

And this is how Pierre begins to disappear from me: I close my eyes and he starts to fade, little by little, to *not be there.* Although I'm lying in his arms, could open my eyes at any time. I keep them closed until more of him is gone, and more and more.

"I am the king of Alfortville," he laughs, which makes me — who, then? Not the queen. His house will be empty of me, soon, empty of my books and notebooks, my footsteps, all my clothes. And then my other life will resume, half a world away. Resume. From the Old French *résumer*, from the Latin, *to take back.*

So we've finished the champagne, repeated all the words we've learned. He's taught me *câlin*, which means caress. And tease: *taquin. Bisou*: a kiss. I've taught him *rare*, as in: that which does not occur very often; and *generous.* "Pierre is generous," I explain. "Pierre is a rich man, very rich." My fist unclenched because I can't hold onto anything. And so.

And so tonight he falls asleep beneath the lamp. I watch him sleep. He's there beside me and he's not. He's dreaming, moving through some other world. We're lost. A stranger smiles across a room. Or steps out of the darkness, startled, asking, "Is it you?"

So that even as he disappears, I disappear from him.

TWO HUNDRED THREE

Morning, already, again. I'm not ready to leave, not yet. But a man I loved once said to me, "If you wait until you're ready, you'll never do anything." That was Pierre. This is Pierre. Waiting now for me at the door.

"Don't cry," he says, as if I might. So I've turned away, at last, and started gathering my bags from the curb in front of the terminal. I assume he's turned away, as well. Gotten into the car and driven off. So I straighten my back in my long black coat, start to walk away, toward my flight.

And then I hear my name being whispered. I hear it clearly, just at my ear. So I turn again and there he is, still half-in and half-out of the car. I drop my bags and rush back to kiss him for the hundred-thousandth time.

"It's hard to say goodbye," he says. Though we've been saying it for hours, since just after dawn, when he woke me with strong black coffee and fresh croissants.

"Which do you want," he asked — *pain aux raisins, pain au chocolat?*

"I want them both," I said. I want to have eaten what was sweetest from his hands. And to have that sweetness, still. And to be flying. Every world.

"Don't be rare," he says. "Susannah, don't be rare." Touches my hair.

quale [kwa-lay]: *Eng.* n 1. A property (such as hardness) considered apart from things that have that property. 2. A property that is experienced as distinct from any source it may have in a physical object. *Ital.* pron.a. 1. Which, what. 2. Who. 3. Some. 4. As, just as.

CPSIA information can be obtained
at www.ICGtesting.com
Printed in the USA
FSOW01n1817140815
9749FS

9 781935 835158